Vipers' Tangle is the supreme example of Mauriac's art. In
all of literature there can be few more appalling studies of
a soul devoured by pride and avarice, corroded by hatred.
The theme of this remarkable novel is the most exciting
in the world—the battle for a human soul.

Louis, the central figure, all but personifies evil. He is a
millionaire many times over, yet wretchedly unhappy. To-
ward the end of his life, seeking to uncover the cause of
his unhappiness, he commits to paper his whole bitter story:
a childhood smothered with indulgence by his mother but
starved of any other affection . . . his love for Isa, and how
it thawed his frozen heart . . . the trivial misunderstanding
that festered until it poisoned their entire married life and
the lives of their children . . . the old miser's struggle to
disinherit his family . . . and the final powerful climax,
with divine grace vying to the very end to pierce the evil
encrusting Louis' soul.

The fascination of this book lies in Mauriac's extraordinary talent for making people live. Probing to the inmost
core of human character, he literally gets inside his subjects.
His genius consists in seeing beneath the surface—far beneath, down to the depths of the soul, where our deepest
selves subsist, where the battle of good and evil wages,
where man's eternal destiny is decided. Subtlety of mind,
clear vision, a sound philosophy of man, and unshakable
honesty in the face of human frailty—these are the sources
of Mauriac's astonishing gift for laying bare the human
heart. Stripping his characters of pretense and mere appearance, he exposes motives mercilessly, yet justly.

Yet this is no picture of unrelieved horror; a deeper,
Catholic dimension—a strain of hope—weaves all through
the story: even Louis can be saved. For what made Louis'
soul a wasteland was lack of love; and Love Himself pur-
sues Louis to the last.

VIPERS' TANGLE

FRANÇOIS MAURIAC
of the French Academy

Translated by
Warre B. Wells

IMAGE BOOKS

A Division of Doubleday & Company, Inc.
Garden City, New York

Cover by Ronald Clyne
Typography by Joseph P. Ascherl

Image Books edition 1957
by special arrangement with Sheed & Ward

Image Books edition published September, 1957

This enemy of his own family, this soul eaten up by hatred and avarice—I would have you, despite his vileness, hold him in pity; I would have him touch your heart. All through his sombre life, dark passions hide from him the light quite near at hand, of which a gleam, sometimes, falls upon him and is on the point of setting him afire—his own passions . . . but, first of all, the indifferent Christians who lie in wait for him, and whom in his turn he tortures. How many of us thus throw the sinner back upon himself, turning him away from a truth which, through our medium, sheds its rays no more!

No, it was not gold that this miser cherished; it was not revenge for which this madman hungered. The real object of his love—you will know it if you have the strength and the courage to bear with this man, even to the moment of his last avowal, cut short by death. . . .

"... Lord, consider that we do not understand ourselves and that we do not know what we would, and that we go infinitely far astray from that which we desire."

SAINT THERESA OF AVILA

PART THE FIRST

Chapter I

YOU will be surprised to find this letter in my safe, lying on top of a packet of securities. It might have been better for me to entrust it to my lawyer, who would have handed it over to you after my death, or else put it in the drawer of my desk—the first drawer that my children will break open before I am even getting cold.

But the fact is that I have gone over this letter in my mind for years and years, and that, when I lie awake, I have always imagined it, all by itself, on the shelf of my safe—an empty safe, containing nothing else but this revenge of mine which, for nearly half a century, I have kept warm.

Don't be afraid. As a matter of fact you are already re-assured. "The securities are there, all right." It seems to me as though I hear that shout of yours, as soon as you are inside the hall, on your return from the bank. Yes, you'll shout to the children: "The securities are there, all right."

It is only by a hair's breadth that they are there. I had laid my plans. If I had chosen, to-day you would be left with nothing except the house and the land. It's lucky for you that I have survived my hatred. For a long time I thought that my hatred was the most alive thing in me—and here I am to-day, at any rate, not even feeling it any longer.

The old man I have become finds it hard to imagine the raging invalid I used to be, who spent his nights, not in-deed in plotting his revenge—that delayed-action bomb was already placed in position, with an attention to detail of which I was proud—but in seeking a way of being able to enjoy it. I wanted to live long enough to see all your faces when you came back from the bank. It was a question of

11

not giving you my authority to open the safe too soon, of giving it to you just late enough for me to have the last joy of hearing you asking in desperation: "Where are the securities?" It seemed to me that then even the most frightful pangs of death could not spoil that pleasure for me.

Yes, I was a man capable of calculating like that. How was I brought to it—a man like myself, who was no monster?

It is four o'clock, and my lunch tray and dirty plates still litter the table, attracting the flies. I have rung in vain; bells never ring in the country. I wait, without impatience, in this room where I slept as a child and where, no doubt, I shall die. The moment I do, the first thought of our daughter Geneviève will be to claim it for the children.

I occupy, all by myself, the largest room, with the best view. Do me the justice of recognising that I offered Geneviève to give it up to her, and that I would have done so, if Doctor Lacaze had not been afraid that the damp of the ground floor would be bad for my bronchitis. Otherwise, no doubt, I should have agreed, but with such resentment that it is lucky I was prevented. (I have spent my whole life making sacrifices whose memory poisoned me, while it fed and fattened those kinds of grudges that time strengthens.)

The taste for squabbling is a family heritage. My father, so I often heard my mother say, quarrelled with his parents, and they died themselves without ever seeing their daughter again since they turned her out thirty years earlier (she founded the family of those Marseilles cousins whom we do not know). We have never known the reason for all this dissension, but we took the hatred of our progenitors on trust; and to this very day I should turn my back on any of those little Marseilles cousins whom I met.

One can avoid seeing his distant relations; one cannot do the same thing with his children, with his wife. There are such things as united families, no doubt; but, when you think of the number of households in which two human beings exasperate one another, disgust one another, at the same table, at the same wash-basin, between the same sheets, it is astonishing how few divorces there are! They detest one another, and still there is no getting away from each other. . . .

What is this fever for writing which has seized upon me to-day, the anniversary of my birth? I am entering upon my sixty-eighth year, and I am the only person who realises it. Geneviève, Hubert, their children, have always, on every anniversary, had their cake, the little candles, flowers. . . .

If I have not given you anything on your birthday for years, it is not because I have forgotten; it is by way of revenge. It suffices. . . . The last bunch of flowers I received on my birthday, my poor mother plucked with her deformed hands. She had dragged herself for the last time, despite her weak heart, as far as the rose-walk.

Where was I? Yes, I am asking you why this sudden frenzy for writing. "Frenzy" is the right word. You can judge it for yourself from my handwriting, from these letters all bent the same way, like pine-trees by the west wind.

Listen: I have told you already about a revenge, long meditated, which I forgo. But there is something in you, something of you, over which I want to triumph. It is your silence.

Oh, don't misunderstand me! You have a well-oiled tongue; you can talk for hours to Cazau about the chickens or the kitchen-garden. With the children, even the smallest of them, you jabber deafeningly all day long. Oh, those meals from which I came away addle-headed, worried as I was by professional cares which I couldn't tell to any-body!—especially after the Villenave case, when I suddenly became a great Assize lawyer, as the papers put it. . . .

No, it is not a question of that now. It is a different kind of silence for which I want to avenge myself: the silence in which you persisted about our marriage, our utter incompatibility. How often, at the theatre, or when I was reading a novel, have I asked myself whether there really are in life mistresses and wives who make "scenes," who explain themselves and open their hearts, who find relief in unburdening themselves?

During the forty years that we have suffered side by side, you have found the strength to avoid a single word that cut the least deep. You have always turned aside.

I thought for a long time that this was deliberate, a matter of policy whose reason escaped me, until at last I realised that, quite simply, it did not interest you. I was so far outside your thoughts that you bolted not from fright, but from boredom. You were clever at scenting my approach, you could see me coming from a distance; and, if I took you by surprise, you fobbed me off easily, or else you patted my cheek, gave me a kiss, and went away.

Perhaps I ought to be afraid that you may tear up this letter after reading the beginning of it; but I'm not, because for some months past I have been a surprise to you. I intrigue you. Little as you observe me, how could you help noticing a change in my mood? Yes, this time I am sure that you will not evade me.

I want you to know, I want you all to know, you, your son, your daughter, your son-in-law, your grandchildren, what he was like—this man who lived alone in the presence of the compact group of you, this over-driven lawyer who had to be taken care of because he held the purse-strings, but who suffered on another planet. What planet? You never chose to go there.

Don't be alarmed—there is no question here of my funeral eulogy written by myself in advance, any more than there is of a tirade against you. The dominant feature of my character, which would have struck any other wife but you, is my frightful lucidity. That skill in deceiving oneself, which helps most men to live, has always been lacking in me. Nothing unpleasant has ever happened to me without my knowing all about it in good time. . . .

I have had to interrupt myself. . . . They did not bring me a lamp; they did not come to close the shutters. I looked at the roof of the wine-vaults, whose tiles have the vivid tints of flowers or birds' breasts. I listened to the thrushes in the ivy and the Carolina poplar, the noise of a cask being rolled.

It is good fortune to await death in the one place in the world where everything remains the same as in my memories. Only the fussing of the motor replaces the creaking of the draw-well which the donkey used to work. (There is also that horrible postal airplane which announces tea-time and defiles the sky.) It does not happen to many men to rediscover in reality, within their range of vision, that world which most find only in themselves, when they have the courage and the patience to remember.

I put my hand to my breast and feel my heart. I look at the glass-fronted cupboard where, in a corner, are the Pravaz syringe, the vial of nitrate of starch—everything that would be necessary in case of a heart attack. Would they hear me if I called? They will have it that it is false *angina pectoris*. They are much less concerned about convincing me than believing it themselves, so that they can sleep undisturbed.

I can breathe better now. One would think it was a hand laid on my left shoulder, holding it cramped and rigid, as someone might do who did not want me to forget. So far as I am concerned, death will not steal upon me like a thief. It has been prowling around me for years. I hear it, I feel its breath. It is patient with me, because I do not defy it, but submit myself to the discipline which its approach imposes.

I contrive to go on living, in a dressing-gown, in the setting of patients suffering from incurable diseases, sunk in the padded arm-chair where my mother awaited her end; sitting, like her, beside a table covered with potions, ill-shaven, ill-smelling, a slave to disgusting habits.

But do not depend on all this. In between my attacks, I

get back into my hide. Lawyer Bourru, who thought me dead, sees me rise again; and I have the strength to go on for hours, in the vaults of safe-deposits, tearing off dividend-warrants for myself.

I must keep alive long enough to finish this confession, so that at last I may make you understand me—you who, during the years when I shared your bed, never failed to tell me at night, the moment I got in: "I'm dropping with sleep, I'm almost asleep already, almost asleep. . . ." What you put aside like this was not nearly so much my caresses as my words.

It is true that our unhappiness had its birth in those endless conversations in which, when we were first married, we delighted to indulge. Two children—I was twenty-three, you eighteen; and perhaps love itself was less of a pleasure to us than these confidences, these intimacies. As children do when they make friends, we had taken a vow to tell each other everything. I, who had so little to confess to you that I had to embellish my poor little adventures, never doubted that you were as badly off as myself. I did not even think that you had ever had another man's name on your lips before mine. I never imagined it, until that night. . . .

It was in this room where I am writing to-day. The wallpaper has been changed; but the mahogany furniture is still in the same position. There was the opaline water-glass on the table and that tea-service won in a lottery. The moonlight flooded the matting. The south wind, coming across the Landes, wafted the scent of a forest fire to our very bed.

That friend of yours, Rodolphe, whom you had often mentioned to me before, and always in the dark in our bedroom, as though his phantom must be present between us at the moments of our deepest union—you spoke his name again that night, do you remember? But that was not enough for you any more.

"There are things I should have told you, my dear, before we became engaged. I feel remorseful because I didn't confess to you. . . . Oh, nothing serious, don't be afraid! . . ."

I was not afraid, and I did nothing to encourage your confession. But you lavished it upon me with a complacency which at first embarrassed me. You were not responding to any prick of conscience. You were not acting in obedience to any sense of what was due to me, as you told me, and as, for that matter, you believed.

No, you were revelling in a delightful memory; you could not hold yourself in any longer. Perhaps you sensed a threat to our happiness in this; but it was, as they say, too much for you. It did not depend upon your will that the shade of that Rodolphe should hover over our bed.

Do not, above all, run away with the belief that our unhappiness had its source in jealousy. I, who was later to become furiously jealous, felt nothing resembling that passion in the course of that summer night about which I am speaking, one night in the year '85, when you confessed to me that at Aix, during the holidays, you had been engaged to that unknown young man.

When I think that only forty-five years later is it given to me to explain myself about this! But will you even read my letter? All this interests you so little! Anything that has to do with me bores you. The children by themselves prevented you from seeing me and understanding me; but after the grandchildren came . . .

No matter: I take this last chance. Perhaps I shall have more authority over you dead than alive—at least during the first few days. For a week or two I shall take a place in your life again. Even if it is only as a matter of duty, you will read these pages to the end. I need to believe that. I do believe it.

Chapter II

NO, I did not feel any jealousy during your confession. How am I to make your understand what it destroyed in me?

I was the only son of that widow whom you knew, or, rather, beside whom you lived for years and years without knowing her. No doubt, even if it had interested you, you would have found it hard to understand what it meant, that union of those two human beings, of that mother and that son—you, a cell in a prosperous, prolific family, of gentle birth, hierarchic, organised. No, you could not conceive what the widow of a modest official, head clerk at the Préfecture, could devote in the way of care to the son who was all that was left to her in the world.

My school successes filled her with pride. They were also my only joy. At that time, I had no doubt about it that we were very poor. The narrowness of our way of life, the strict economy which my mother made a law to herself, sufficed to convince me of the fact. It is true that I lacked for nothing. I realise to-day how far I was a spoilt child.

My mother's farm at Hosteins provided fare cheaply for our table, and I should have been very much surprised if anybody had told me that it was very good food. Chickens fattened on barley, hares, wood-cock *pâté*, awakened in me no idea of luxury. I had always heard that our land was not worth very much.

As a matter of fact, when my mother inherited the property, it consisted of an untilled stretch of country where my grandfather, as a child, had himself taken cattle to graze. What I did not know was that my parents had made it their first business to develop it, and that, when I came to the age of twenty-one, I should find myself the owner of two thousand hectares of maturing timber, which was already providing pit-props.

Besides, my mother saved out of her modest income. Even while my father was still alive, by dint of "bleeding themselves white" they had bought Calèse—for forty thousand francs: that vineyard which to-day I wouldn't let go for a million! We lived in the Rue Sainte Catherine, on the third floor of a house which belonged to us. (Together with some undeveloped building land, it constituted my father's inheritance.) Twice a week a hamper arrived from the country. My mother went to the butcher's as little as possible.

As for me, I lived in the fixed idea of the Teachers' Training College which I proposed to enter. It was a hard job to make me "take the air" on Thursdays and Sundays. I was not in the least like those children who are always first in class and pretend that they do it without taking any trouble. I was a "swotter," and I prided myself upon it: a swotter, and nothing else. I don't remember ever having found the least pleasure at school in studying Virgil or Racine. All this was merely the raw material of examinations.

Out of the Humanities I isolated those subjects which were on my lecture courses—the only subjects which had any importance in my eyes—and about them I wrote what one required to write to satisfy the examiners: in other words, what had already been said and written by generations of candidates.

That was the kind of idiot I was, and such, perhaps, I should have remained, but for my hæmoptysis, which terrified my mother and, two months before the Training College examination, compelled me to give up everything.

It was the price I had to pay for too studious a childhood and an unhealthy adolescence. A growing boy cannot with impunity live bent over a table, with his shoulders hunched together, until a late hour of the night, despising any kind of physical exercise.

Am I boring you? I tremble at the idea of boring you. But don't skip a line. Be assured that I am sticking to essentials. The tragedy of our two lives hung upon these events, about which you knew nothing, or which you have forgotten.

In any case you can see, from these first few pages, that I don't propose to spare myself. There is matter here to flatter your hatred. . . . No, don't protest: when you think of me, it is to nourish your enmity.

I am afraid, though, of being unjust towards the puny little boy that I was, leaning over his dictionaries. When I read other people's memories of their childhood, when I see that Paradise on which they look back, I ask myself with a pang:

"And what about me? Why this dead level from the very beginning of my life? Perhaps I have forgotten what others remember; perhaps I knew the same enchantments."

Alas! I can see nothing but that desperate striving for the first place, nothing but my envious rivalry with one fellow called Henoch and another called Rodrigue. My instinct led me to repulse any attraction. The prestige of my success, and even my surliness, drew certain types of characters towards me, I remember. I was a fierce child towards anybody who wanted to make friends with me. I had a horror of "sentimentality."

If writing were my profession, I could not extract out of my schoolboy's life a single touching page. But wait a minute . . . there was one thing, perhaps—next to nothing: my father, whom I barely remembered. Sometimes it happened that I persuaded myself that he was not dead, that a combination of strange circumstances had made him disappear.

When I returned home from school, I went up the Rue Sainte Catherine at a run, in the road, dodging about through the traffic, because the crowds on the pavement would have held me up. I took the stairs four at a time.

My mother was mending linen at the window. My father's photograph hung in its usual place, to the right of the bed. I let my mother kiss me, barely returning her kiss; I was already opening my books.

As the sequel to that hæmoptysis which changed my fate, melancholy months went by in that cottage at Arcachon where the ruin of my health consummated the shipwreck of my university ambitions. My poor mother irritated me because to her this did not count, and she seemed to me to care little about my future.

Every day she lived in expectation of "thermometer time." Upon my weekly weighing depended all her sorrow or all her joy. I, who was later to suffer so much from being ill without my illness interesting anybody, can recognise that I was justly punished for my hardness, my irreconcilability, as a boy only too much loved.

With the first fine weather I "came out on top," as my mother put it. Indeed, I came to life again. I grew taller and stronger. My body, which had suffered so much from the régime under which I had distorted it, bloomed in the dry forest, full of broom and arbutus, at that time when Arcachon was only a village.

It was then, too, that I learnt from my mother that I had no occasion to worry about the future, that we had a handsome fortune which was growing year by year. There was no need for me to hurry—especially as I should probably be exempted from my military service. I had a great fluency of speech which had struck all my masters. My mother wanted me to study law, and she had no doubt that, without too much trouble, I should become a famous barrister, unless politics attracted me. . . .

She talked and talked, telling me all her plans at once; and I listened to her, sulky, hostile, looking out of the window.

I was beginning to be "fast." My mother watched me with fearful indulgence. Since then, while living with your people, I have observed how much importance is attached to such irregularities in a religious family. My mother, for her part, saw nothing wrong about them except in so far as they might injure my health. Once she was assured that I did not overdo things, she shut her eyes to my nocturnal excursions, so long as I was home by midnight.

No, don't be afraid that I am going to tell you about my love affairs of that time. I know you have a horror of such things, and, besides, they were such mean little adventures!

All the same, I had to pay for them. They made me suffer. I suffered because there was so little charm about me that my youth was no good to me. Not that I was ugly, I think. My features are "regular," and Geneviève, my living image, turned out a lovely girl. But I belonged to that race of beings of whom it is said that they have no youth: only a dreary adolescence, with no freshness about it.

I chilled people, just by the look of me. The more I realised it, the stiffer I got. I never knew how to dress myself, how to choose a tie, or how to knot it. I was never able to let myself go, or laugh, or play the fool. It was unimaginable that I should join any gang of bright young people; I belonged to the race of those whose presence spoils everything.

Besides, I was sensitive, incapable of taking the slightest joke. On the other hand, when I tried to make a joke myself, I wounded people in a way for which they never forgave me. I went straight to the sore spot, to the infirmity, about which one should keep his mouth shut.

With women, through shyness and self-consciousness, I assumed that superior, magisterial tone which they abominate. I never could admire their frocks. The more I felt that they disliked me, the more I exaggerated everything about me that made me a horror to them. My youth was nothing but one long suicide. I hastened to displease on purpose for fear of displeasing naturally.

Rightly or wrongly, I blamed my mother for what I was. I felt that I was expiating the misfortune of having been, even since I was a child, excessively brooded over and supervised and attended. I was frightfully hard with her at that time. I reproached her with the excess of her love. I did not pardon her for what she was to prove the only person in the world to give me—for what I was never to know except through her.

Forgive me for going back on this; but it is in this thought that I find the strength to bear the loneliness to which you have condemned me. It is only fair that I should pay. Poor woman, asleep these many years, whose memory survives only in the worn-out heart of an old man like myself—how she would have suffered, if she could have foreseen how Fate would avenge her!

Yes, I was cruel. In the little dining-room of our cottage, under the hanging lamp that lit our meals, I answered her timid questions only with monosyllables; or else I lost my temper outrageously on the least pretext or for no reason at all.

She did not try to understand. She did not go into the reasons for my rages; she submitted to them as to the wrath of God. It was my illness, she used to say; I must not let my nerves get out of order. She added that she was too ignorant to understand me. "I know that an old woman like me isn't very good company for a boy of your age." She, whom I had always found so economical, not to say miserly, gave me more money than I asked for, encouraged me to spend it, and brought me back from Bordeaux preposterous ties which I refused to wear.

We made the acquaintance of some neighbours, whose daughter I courted—not that I was in love with her. She was spending the winter at Arcachon for the sake of her health, and my mother was obsessed with the idea of possible contagion, or of my compromising her and becoming engaged despite myself. I am quite sure to-day that I devoted myself to this conquest—to no purpose, for that matter—simply to hurt my mother.

We went back to Bordeaux after a year of absence. We had moved. My mother had bought a house on the boulevards, but she had said nothing about it to me in order to keep it a surprise for me. I was astonished when a footman opened the door to us.

The first floor was reserved for me. Everything seemed to be new. Secretly dazzled though I was by a display of wealth which I imagine to-day must have been in frightful taste, I was cruel enough to do nothing but make criticisms and worry about the money that it must have cost.

It was then that my mother triumphantly gave me an accounting—which, as a matter of fact, was not due to me, since the bulk of the fortune came from her family. Fifty thousand francs a year, without reckoning timber-felling, constituted at that time, especially in the provinces, a "pretty" fortune, of which any other fellow would have taken advantage to raise himself to the highest society in the town.

It was by no means ambition in which I was lacking; but I was unable to hide from my comrades at the Faculty of Law my unfriendly feelings towards them. They were almost all sons of leading families, educated by the Jesuits. Grammar-school boy and grandson of a shepherd as I was, I could not forgive them for the horrible feeling of envy which their manners inspired in me, although they struck me as my inferiors from the point of view of brains. To envy people one despises—there is enough in that shameful passion to poison a whole life.

I envied them and I despised them; and their contempt for me—which perhaps I imagined—increased my resentment all the more. Such was my nature that I did not think for a moment of winning them over.

I plunged deeper every day into association with their adversaries. Hatred of religion, which has so long been my dominating passion, which made you suffer so much and rendered us mortal enemies—this hatred had its birth at the Faculty of Law, in 1879 and in 1880, at the time of the vote on Article 7, the year of the famous decrees and of the expulsion of the Jesuits.

Until then I had lived indifferent to these questions. My mother never talked about them except to say: "I don't worry; if people like ourselves are not saved, there's no hope for anybody." She had me baptised. My first Communion at school struck me as a boring formality, of which I retained only a confused memory. In any case, it was not followed by any other.

My ignorance of these matters was profound. Priests in the street, when I was a child, seemed to me like persons in disguise, masqueraders of some kind. I never thought about problems of this nature, and, when I finally approached them, it was from the political point of view.

I founded a study circle which met at the Café Voltaire, where I practised as a speaker. Shy though I was in private life, I became another man in public debate. I had followers, and I enjoyed being their leader; but fundamentally I despised them no less than the upper classes. I blamed them for exhibiting their petty motives so simple-mindedly. These motives were also my own, and they forced me to recognise the fact.

Sons of minor officials, winners of scholarships, clever and ambitious fellows but full of spleen, they flattered me without being fond of me. Once or twice I invited them to meals, which constituted occasions that they talked about long afterwards. But their manners sickened me. I got to the point where I could not refrain from gibes which wounded them mortally and gave them a grudge against me.

Nevertheless my anti-religious hatred was sincere. A certain desire for social justice tormented me too. I compelled my mother to knock down the mud huts where our farm labourers lived, badly nourished on sour wine and black bread. For the first time she tried to oppose me. "For all the gratitude they'll show you . . ."

But I went no further. I suffered through my recognition of the fact that my adversaries and myself had a common passion: land, money. There were the "haves," and there were the "have-nots." I realised that I should always be on the side of the possessors.

My fortune was equal or superior to that of all these stuck-up fellows who, as I imagined, turned their heads away when they saw me—though doubtless they would not have refused the offer of my hand. Besides, people were not lacking, on the Right and on the Left, who reproached me at public meetings with my two thousand hectares of timber and my vineyards.

Forgive me for lingering over all this. But, if I did not go into these details, perhaps you would not understand what our meeting meant to such a sore-head as I was, and what our love meant. I, son of peasants, whose mother had "worn the kerchief," marry a demoiselle Fondaudège! It surpassed imagination, it was unimaginable. . . .

Chapter III

I stopped writing because the light was getting dim, and because I heard talking underneath me. Not that all of you were making much noise—on the contrary, you were talking in low voices, and that was what disturbed me. Once, from this room, I could follow your conversations. But now you are suspicious; you whisper.

You told me the other day that I was getting hard of hearing. Not at all: I can hear the rumbling of the train on the viaduct. No, no, I'm not deaf. It is you who lower your voices and do not want me to catch what you are saying.

What are you hiding from me? Business going badly, eh? And there they all are round you, with their tongues hanging out: the son-in-law who deals in rum and the grandson-in-law who does nothing, and our son Hubert, the stockbroker. . . . Hasn't he got the money of the whole world at his disposal, this fellow who pays twenty per cent?

Don't count on me. I'm not going to let the titbit go. "It would be so easy to fell the pines . . ." you are going to suggest to me this evening. You will remind me that Hubert's two daughters have been living with their people-in-law since they got married, because they have no money to furnish. "We have heaps of furniture in the attic going to loss; it wouldn't cost us anything to lend them some. . . ."

That's what you are going to tell me, a little later. "They're angry with us about it. They never set foot here now. I'm deprived of my own grandchildren." That's what you are all discussing; that's what you are talking about in low voices.

I read over these lines which I wrote yesterday evening in a kind of delirium. How could I have let my temper carry me away like that? This is not a letter any more; it is a diary, interrupted, begun again. . . .

Shall I rub all that out? Make a fresh start? Impossible. Time presses. What I have written is written.

Besides, what do I want to do, if not strip myself before you utterly, compel you to see me just as I am? For the last thirty years I have been nothing more in your eyes than a machine for handing out thousand-franc notes: a machine that works badly and that you have to keep on shaking, until the time comes when you can at last open it, tear the inside out of it, grab by the handful at the treasures it contains.

Again I'm letting my temper get the better of me. It brings me back to the point where I broke off. I must go back to the origin of this rage, recall that fatal night. . . . But first of all, remember how we met.

I was at Luchon, with my mother, in August '85. The Hotel Sacarron at that time was full of padded furniture, stuffed hassocks and izards. The lime-trees in the Allées d'Etigny—it is still their scent that I smell, after all these years, when the lime-trees flower. The staccato trot of donkeys, the tinkling of bells, the cracking of whips awakened me in the morning. The water of the mountains murmured in the very streets. Vendors cried *croissants* and milk-loaves. Guides went by on horseback, and I watched cavalcades setting out.

All the first floor was occupied by the Fondaudèges. They had King Leopold's suite. "Must have plenty of money to spend, those people!" my mother used to say. That did not stop them always being behindhand when it was a question of paying (they had rented some extensive ground which we owned at the docks, to tranship merchandise).

We dined at the common table; but you Fondaudèges

ate by yourselves. I remember that round table, near the windows, and that obese grandmother of yours, who hid her bald skull under black lace from which jet dangled. I always used to think that she was smiling at me; but it was the shape of her tiny eyes and the disproportionate gap of her mouth which created this illusion. A nun waited upon her, with a bloated, bilious face, swathed in starched linen.

Your mother—how beautiful she was! Clad in black, in perpetual mourning for her two lost children. It was she, and not you, whom I first admired, furtively. The bareness of her neck, arms and hands disturbed me. She wore no jewelry. I imagined Stendhalian summonses, and gave myself until the evening to speak to her or slip a letter to her.

As for you, I hardly noticed you. I thought that girls did not interest me. Besides, you had that insolent air of never looking at other people, which is one way of suppressing them.

One day, when I came back from the Casino, I surprised my mother in conversation with Madame Fondaudège. She was being too condescending, too friendly, like somebody who despaired of lowering herself to the level of her companion. On the contrary, Mamma was taking a haughty tone; this was a tenant whom she had between her paws, and the Fondaudèges were nothing more in her eyes than negligent debtors. A peasant, a landowner, she distrusted commerce and its fragile, perhaps fleeting fortunes. I interrupted her as she was saying: "Of course, I trust Monsieur Fondaudège's signature, but . . ."

For the first time I took part in a business conversation. Madame Fondaudège obtained the delay in payment that she wanted.

I have very often thought, since then, that my mother's peasant instinct did not mislead her. Your family has cost me dearly enough, and, if I had let myself be devoured, your son, your daughter, your grandson-in-law would soon have annihilated my fortune and swallowed it up in their business. Those businesses of theirs! A first-floor office, a telephone, a typist. . . . Behind this setting, money disappears by the hundred-thousands.

But I digress. . . . We are in 1885, at Bagnères-de-Luchon.

Now I saw this influential family smiling at me. Your grandmother never stopped talking, because she was deaf. But when I had a chance of exchanging a few words with your mother, after meals, she bored me and upset the romantic ideas which I had formed about her. You will not be angry with me if I recall that her conversation was banal, and that she inhabited a world so limited, and used a vocabulary so restricted, that at the end of three minutes I was in despair of carrying on the conversation.

My attention, turned away from the mother, devoted itself to the daughter. I did not realise all at once that no obstacle was put in the way of our intercourse. How should I have imagined that the Fondaudèges saw a good match in me?

I remember a drive in the valley of the Lys: your grandmother on the back seat of the victoria, with the nun; and we two on the bracket-seat. God knows there were carriages enough in Luchon! One had to be a Fondaudège to bring one's own turn-out.

The horses went at a walk, in a cloud of flies. The Sister's face shone; her eyes were half-closed. Your grandmother fanned herself with a fan, bought in the Allées d'Etigny, on which was designed a matador giving the death-thrust to a black bull. You were wearing long gloves, in spite of the heat. Everything you had on you was white, down to your high-legged boots.

You were "devoted to white," you told me, since the death of your two brothers. I did not know what "devoted to white" meant. I have learned, since, what a taste your family has for these rather odd devotions. Such was my state of mind that I found that highly poetical.

How can I make you understand what you aroused in me? All at once I had the feeling that I was no longer displeasing; I had ceased to repel, I was not hateful. One of the most important dates in my life was that evening when you said to me:

"It's extraordinary for a man to have such long lashes."

I carefully concealed my advanced ideas. I remember how, during that drive, the two of us got out to lighten the carriage up a hill, and your grandmother and the nun said their rosary, and from the top of his box-seat the old coachman, trained for years, responded to the *Ave Maria*. You looked at me with a smile yourself; but I kept a straight face.

It cost me nothing to accompany you to eleven o'clock Mass on Sundays. For me no metaphysical idea was attached to this ceremony. It was the form of worship of a class, to which I was proud to feel myself admitted; a kind of religion of ancestors for the use of the upper classes, a body of ritual lacking any significance other than social.

Because, sometimes, you looked at me sidelong, the memory of those Masses remains associated with that marvellous discovery which I was in process of making: I was capable of interesting, of pleasing, of exciting. The love that I felt was merged with the love that I inspired—that I believed I inspired. My own feelings had nothing real about them. What counted was my faith in the love which you had for me.

I saw my own reflection in another human being; and my image, thus reflected, had nothing repulsive about it. I stretched my petals with a delightful sense of relaxing. I remember that thawing of my whole personality under the warmth of your eyes, that gushing of emotions, that unbinding of springs. The most ordinary little expressions of affection, a handshake, a flower pressed in a book—everything was new to me, everything enchanted me.

Only my mother did not reap the benefit of this renewal of myself—in the first place because I felt that she was hostile to the dream (which I thought mad) that was slowly taking shape within me. I was angry with her because she was not dazzled. "Don't you see that these people are try-ing to attract you?" she kept on saying, without any idea that she was thus running the risk of destroying my im-mense joy in having at last found favour in a girl's eyes.

There really did exist in the world a girl who liked me, and perhaps wanted to marry me. I believed it, despite my mother's distrust; for your family was too big, too influen-tial, to find any advantage in an alliance with us. That did not stop my cherishing a resentment, bordering on hatred, towards my mother, because she put my happiness in doubt.

Nor did that stop her making inquiries through her sources of information in the leading banks. It was a tri-umph for me when she had to admit that the Fondaudège business, despite a temporary embarrassment, was in a very strong credit position. "They make any amount of money, but they live in too much style," said Mamma. "Everything goes into stables and livery. They prefer to throw dust in people's eyes, rather than lay aside. . . ."

The banks' information rounded off my assurance of my happiness. I had proof of your people's disinterestedness; they smiled upon me because they liked me. Suddenly it seemed to me quite natural that everybody should like me. They used to leave me alone with you in the evening in the walks of the Casino.

How strange it is that, at those beginnings of life when a little happiness is handed out to us, there is no voice which warns us: "However old you may live to be, you will never have any other joy in the world than these few hours. Savour them to the very dregs, because, after this, there is nothing left for you. This first spring on which you have stumbled is also the last. Quench your thirst, once and for all; you shall not drink again."

But I was persuaded, on the contrary, that this was the beginning of a long, impassioned life; and I did not pay enough heed to those evenings that we spent, not stirring, under the sleeping leaves.

Nevertheless there were signs; but I interpreted them badly. Do you remember that night when we were sitting on a bench, on the path that winds up behind the Baths? Suddenly, for no apparent reason, you burst into tears. I recall the scent of your wet cheeks, the scent of that grief without a name. I believed in the tears of happy love. My youth was unable to interpret those sobs, those chokings. It is true that you said to me:

"It isn't anything—it's just being with you."

You were not lying, you liar. It was, indeed, because you were with me that you cried—with me and not with somebody else; not with the man whose name you were at last to confess to me, some months later, in this room where I am writing: I, an old man near death, amid a family on the alert, awaiting the moment of the kill.

And I, on that bench on the winding path of Superbagnères—I nestled my face in between your shoulder and your neck, and breathed in that little girl in tears. The moist, warm Pyrenean night, which smelt of damp grass and mint, had acquired something of the scent of you as well. In the Place des Thermes, on which we looked down, the foliage of the lime-trees around the bandstand gleamed with the lamps. An old Englishman, staying at the hotel, was catching with a long net the moths that they lured.

You said to me: "Lend me your handkerchief." I dried your eyes, and tucked that handkerchief away between my shirt and my heart.

It is not too much to say that I had become another man. Even my face—a light had touched it. I knew it by the way in which women looked at me. No suspicion came to me, after that night of tears.

Besides, for one night like that, how many were there when you were sheer joy; when you leant against me, when you clung to my arm? I walked too fast for you, and you panted to keep up with me.

I was a chaste lover. You appealed to an intact part of me. Never once was I tempted to take advantage of the trust which your people placed in me. I was a thousand miles from believing that it could be calculated.

Yes, I was another man, to such a point that one day . . . Forty years afterwards, I finally pluck up courage to make this confession to you. It will not give you the taste of triumph now, when you read this letter.

It was one day on the road through the Lys valley. We had got out of the victoria. The waters murmured. I rubbed fennel between my hands. Night was gathering at the foot of the mountains, but on the summits light was still encamped. . . .

I suddenly had an intense feeling, an almost physical certitude, that another world existed, a reality of which we knew nothing but the shadow. . . .

It was only for an instant—an instant which, in the course of my sad life, has repeated itself, at very long intervals. But its very rarity gives it an enhanced value in my eyes. And so, later on, during the long religious strife that tore us asunder, I had to brush away that memory. . . .

This is a confession which I owe you. But it is not time yet to touch upon this subject.

It is unnecessary to recall our engagement. It was arranged one evening; and it took place without my intending that it should. You interpreted, I think, something I said in quite a different sense from what I meant. I found myself bound to you, and I let it go at that. It is unnecessary to recall all this. But there was something horrible on which my mind is condemned to rest.

You informed me of one of your conditions at once. "In the interests of good understanding," you refused to have a common household with my mother, or even to live in the same house. Your parents and yourself had made up your minds to have no compromise about this.

After all these years, how vividly it remains present in my memory—that stifling hotel room, that window open on the Allées d'Etigny! Golden dust, the cracking of whips, the sound of bells, a Tyrolean air came in through the closed shutters.

My mother, who had a headache, was lying on the sofa, in skirt and camisole—she had never had such a thing as a wrap, a peignoir, or a dressing-gown. I took advantage of her saying that she would leave us the lower rooms and content herself with one on the third floor.

"Listen, Mother. Isa thinks that it would be better . . ."

As I spoke, I looked at that old face furtively; and then I turned my eyes away. With her deformed fingers, Mother was plucking at the frill of her camisole. If she had protested, I should have known how to take it; but her silence did not encourage anger.

She pretended not to be hurt, or even surprised. Finally she spoke, choosing words which might make me believe that she had been expecting our separation.

"I shall live most of the year at Aurigne," she said; "it is the most habitable of our farms, and I'll leave you Calèse. I shall have a bungalow built at Aurigne; three rooms will be enough for me. It won't cost much, but, even so, it's annoying to go to this expense, when I may be dead next year. But you can use it later on, for the pigeon-shooting. You yourself don't like shooting but you may have children with a taste for it."

However far my ingratitude might go, it was impossible to come to the end of that love of hers. Dislodged from its position, it re-established itself elsewhere. It organised itself with what I left it, and made the best of it. But, that evening, you asked me:

"What's the matter with your mother?"

She recovered her normal appearance the very next day. Your father arrived from Bordeaux with his elder daughter and his son-in-law. They must have been kept informed. They looked me up and down. I imagined I could hear them asking one another:

"Do you think he's 'eligible'? The mother's impossible."

I shall never forget how surprised I was to see your sister Marie Louise, whom you called Marinette, your elder by a year, but looking younger than you, a slim girl, with that long neck, that too heavy chignon, and those infantile eyes of hers. The old man to whom your father had handed her over, Baron Philipot, filled me with horror. But, since his death, I have often thought of that sexagenarian as one of the most unhappy men I have ever known. What a martyrdom that idiot suffered, to try and make his young wife forget that he was an old man!

A corset pressed him to suffocation-point. His starched collar, high and wide, juggled away his jowls and dewlaps. The shining dye of his moustache and whiskers accentuated the purple of his ravaged face. He scarcely listened to what anybody said to him, and was always looking for a mirror; and, when he found one, don't you remember our smiles when we surprised the glance which the unhappy man gave his image: that perpetual examination which he imposed on himself?

His false teeth prevented him from smiling. His lips were sealed by an unfailing will. We used to make remarks, too, about the way in which he put on his Kronstadt hat, so as not to disarrange that extraordinary strand of hair, starting at his nape, which scattered over his skull like the delta of a river in low water.

Your father, who was his contemporary, despite his white beard, his baldness and his stomach, still pleased the ladies. Even in his business he set himself to charm. Only my mother resisted him. Perhaps the blow which I had just given her had hardened her. She discussed every clause of the marriage settlement as she would have done in the case of a sale or a lease. I pretended to be indignant over her stiffness and disowned her—secretly glad to know that my interests were in such good hands.

If my fortune is to-day completely separate from yours, if you have so little hold upon me, I owe it to my mother, who demanded the most drastic system of settlement, as though I were a girl resolved to marry a debauchee. So long as the Fondaudèges did not draw back before her demands, I could sleep with an easy mind. They stuck to me, I thought, because you stuck to me.

Mamma would not hear of an annual income; she insisted that your dowry should be paid in cash.

"They hold up to me the example of Baron Philipot," she said, "who took the elder daughter without a halfpenny. . . . I dare say! To give that poor girl to that old man they must have got something out of it! But we're another matter. They thought that I should be dazzled by their alliance. They don't know me. . . ."

We "turtle-doves" pretended to take no interest in the discussion. I imagine that you had as much confidence in your father's shrewdness as I had in my mother's. And after all, perhaps we did not know, either of us, how very fond of money we were. . . .

No, I'm unfair. You were never fond of it except for your children's sake. You would kill me, perhaps, to enrich them; but you would take the bread out of your own mouth for them.

While I . . . I am fond of money, I admit. It comforts me. So long as I remain master of my fortune, you can do nothing against me.

"We need so little at our age," you keep on telling me. How wrong you are! An old man only lives by virtue of what he possesses. Once he ceases to possess anything, he is thrown on the scrap-heap. We have only the choice between the almshouse, the workhouse, and our fortunes. Those stories of peasants who let their old relations die of hunger after robbing them of everything—how often have I stumbled on the equivalent, with a little more form and ceremony, in upper-class families!

Yes, indeed, I am afraid of being poor. I feel as though I could never accumulate enough money. It attracts you; but it protects me.

The hour of the Angelus has passed, and I have not heard it. . . . But it hasn't been rung: to-day is Good Friday. The men of the family are motoring here this evening. I shall go down to dinner. I want to see them all together. I feel stronger against all of them than when I talk to them separately.

Besides, I insist on eating my cutlet, on this day of penitence—not out of bravado, but to show all of you that I have kept my strength of will intact and that I shall not give way on any point.

All the positions which I have occupied for the past forty-five years, and from which you have failed to dislodge me, would fall one by one if I made a single concession. In the face of this family feeding itself on haricot beans and sardines in oil, my Good Friday cutlet will be the sign that there is no hope of despoiling me while I am still alive.

Chapter IV

I was quite right. My presence in your midst, yesterday evening, upset your plans. They were happy only at the children's table because, on Good Friday evening, they were dining on chocolate and bread and butter. I cannot tell them one from another: my grand-daughter Janine already has a child old enough to walk. . . .

I regaled them all with the spectacle of an excellent appetite. You made allusion to my state of health and my great age, by way of excusing the cutlet in the eyes of the children.

What struck me as rather terrible was Hubert's optimism. He said that he was sure stocks would go up soon, with the air of a man to whom it was a question of life or death. After all, he is my son. This man in his forties is my son; I know it, but I don't feel it. It is impossible to look a truth like that in the face.

Still, if his business should go wrong! A stockbroker who pays such dividends plays for high stakes and takes big risks. . . . If a day comes when the honour of the family is at stake . . .

The honour of the family! There's an idol to which I am not going to sacrifice. Let me make up my mind firmly in advance. I must stand up to them and not get sentimental —especially as there is always old uncle Fondaudège, who will come into action if I don't. . . .

But I am straying from the point, I'm rambling . . . or, rather, I am shirking the summons of that night when, unknown to yourself, you destroyed our happiness.

It is strange to think that probably you do not even remember it. Those few hours of warm darkness, in this room, decided our two fates. Every word you said separated them a little more; and you had no idea of it. Your memory, stuffed with futile recollections by the thousand, has retained nothing of that disaster.

Bear in mind that from your point of view, as one who professes to believe in eternal life, it was my eternity itself which you staked and compromised that night. For our love at the beginning had made me sensitive to the atmosphere of faith and worship which bathed your life. I loved you, and I loved the spiritual part of your personality. I was touched when you knelt down in your long schoolgirl's nightgown. . . .

We slept in this room where I am writing these lines. Why, on our return from our honeymoon, did we come here to Calèse to stay with my mother? (I had refused to let her give us Calèse, which was her own creation and which she loved.) I have remembered since, to feed my resentment, some circumstances which at first escaped me, or to which I closed my eyes.

In the first place, your people seized upon the death of an uncle once removed as a pretext for a quiet wedding. It is obvious that they were ashamed of such a modest alliance. Baron Philipot was telling everybody how, at Bagnères-de-Luchon, his little sister-in-law had "fallen for" a young man who was attractive enough, with a future before him, and very rich, but of obscure origin.

"In short," he said, "he has no birth." He talked about me as though I were an illegitimate child. On the whole, however, he found it a good thing that I had no family to make one blush. My old mother was, after all, presentable, and she seemed to know how to keep her place. Finally, according to him, you were a spoilt little girl who did what she liked with her parents; and my fortune was respectable enough to persuade the Fondaudèges to consent to this marriage and shut their eyes to everything else.

When this gossip came to my ears, it told me nothing

that, as a matter of fact, I did not know already. Happiness distracted me from attaching any importance to it; and I am bound to say that, on my own side, I found this almost clandestine wedding to my advantage.

Where could I have found groomsmen in the little starveling crew of which I had been the leader? My pride prevented me from making advances to my former enemies. This brilliant marriage would have made reconciliation with them easy; but I am blackening myself enough in this confession not to need to disguise this trait of my character: independence, inflexibility. I bow down to nobody. I remain faithful to my ideas.

On this point my marriage awakened some remorse in me. I had promised your parents to do nothing to turn you away from your religious observances, but I gave no undertaking on my own side except that I would not join the Freemasons. For that matter, your family did not dream of asking anything more of me. At that time religion did not concern anybody but women. In your world, a husband "accompanied his wife to Mass": that was the accepted formula. At Luchon I had already shown your family that I had no objection to that.

When we came back from Venice, in September '85, your parents found various pretexts for not receiving us at their château of Cenon, where their friends and those of the Philipots left no vacant room. We discovered, therefore, that it would be to our advantage to go and stay for the time being with my mother. The recollection of our harshness towards her did not embarrass us in the least. We arranged to live with her as long as it suited us.

She was careful not to "crow over us." The house was ours, she said. We could entertain whom we liked. She would keep to herself, and nobody need see her. She said: "I know how to keep out of the way." She also said: "I'm out of doors most of the time." As a matter of fact, she kept herself very busy with the vines, the cellar, the poultry and the laundry. After meals, she went up to her room for a little, and excused herself when she joined us in the drawing-room. She knocked before she came in, and I had to tell her that that was not done.

She even went so far as to offer to let you do the house-keeping; but you spared her that mortification. For that matter, you had no desire to undertake it. Oh, your condescension towards her; and what humble gratitude she showed you!

You did not separate me from her as much as she had feared. I even showed myself pleasanter to her than before our marriage. The way we used to laugh surprised her. This happy young husband was really her son, who used to be so reserved, so hard. She had not known how to take me, she thought. You were making good the harm she had done.

I remember her admiration when you daubed paint on fans and tambourines, when you sang, or when you played on the piano, always pedalling at the same places, a *Song without Words* of Mendelssohn.

Girl friends of yours came to see you sometimes. You used to tell them: "You must see my mother-in-law, she's a character, a real country lady—they don't exist now." You discovered that she had a lot of "style." She had a way of talking patois to her servants which you thought very smart. You even went so far as to exhibit the daguerreotype of Mamma, at the age of fifteen, still wearing the kerchief. You quoted a couplet about the old peasant families, "more noble than plenty of nobles."

How conventional you were at that time! It was maternity that made you natural again.

I still recoil from the story of that night. It was so hot that we could not keep the shutters closed, despite your horror of bats.

We knew very well that it was the rustling of the leaves of a lime-tree against the house; but still it seemed to us as though somebody were breathing at the other end of the room. Sometimes the wind in the leaves imitated the sound of rain. The moon, in its setting, lit up the floor and the pale phantoms of our clothes lying about. We had ceased to hear the rustling of the meadow, whose murmur had died away.

You said to me: "Let's go to sleep. We must get to sleep." But over our weariness a shadow hovered. We had not come up alone from the depths of the abyss. He rose up too, that unknown Rodolphe, whom I awakened in your heart as soon as my arms closed around you.

And when I opened them again, we sensed his presence. I did not want to suffer. I was afraid of suffering. The instinct of self-preservation applies to happiness too. I knew that I ought not to question you. I let that name burst like a bubble on the surface of our life. What slept beneath the sleeping waters, that principle of corruption, that rotten secret—I did nothing to stir it from its source.

But you, wretched woman—you felt a need of words to liberate that disappointed passion which had remained hungry. A single question that escaped me sufficed.

"Well, this Rodolphe of yours—who was he?"

"It's something I should have told you. . . . Oh, nothing serious, don't be afraid."

You spoke in a low, hurried voice. Your head was no longer lying on my shoulder. Already the infinitesimal space that separated our outstretched bodies had become impassable.

The son of an Austrian mother and a big industrialist of the North. . . . You had met him at Aix, where you had gone with your grandmother, the year before our meeting at Luchon. He had just left Cambridge. You did not describe him to me, but I at once attributed to him all the graces which I knew I lacked. The moonlight on the bed lit up my big, knotted peasant's hand, with its short nails.

You had done nothing really wrong, though he was, you told me, less respectful than I had been. My memory has retained no details of your confession. What did it matter to me? It was not a question of that. If you had not loved him, I could have consoled myself for one of those passing weaknesses in which a child's purity suddenly collapses.

But already I was asking myself: "Less than a year after this great love, how could she have loved me?" Terror froze me.

"It was all a sham," I said to myself. "She lied to me. I am not set free. How could I have thought that any girl would fall in love with me? I am a man whom nobody can love."

The stars were twinkling before the dawn. A blackbird awakened. The breath of wind that we heard in the leaves, long before we felt it on our bodies, filled the curtains and bathed my eyes, as in the days when I was happy. That happiness had existed ten minutes ago—and already I was thinking: "In the days when I was happy. . . ." I put a question.

"He didn't want to marry you?"

You kicked against the pricks of that, I remember. I still have in my ears the special voice that you put on then, when your vanity was in question. Of course, on the contrary he had been very much in love with you, and would have been very proud to marry a Fondaudège. But his parents had learned that you had lost two brothers, both carried away when they were adolescent by consumption. As his own health was not good, his family was immovable.

I questioned you calmly. Nothing warned you what you were in process of destroying.

"All this, my dear, was providential for the two of us," you told me. "You know how proud my parents are—rather ridiculous, I know. I may as well tell you: for our happiness to become possible, it was necessary that this marriage that didn't come off should stick in their heads. You don't know how much importance is attached in our world to anything that has to do with health, once it is a question of marriage. Mamma imagined that the whole town knew all about my misadventure. Nobody would ever want to marry me again. She had the fixed idea that I should be an old maid. What a life she led me for the next few months! As if I hadn't enough to bear with my own disappointment. . . . She ended by persuading us, both Papa and me, that I was not 'marriageable.'"

I refrained from saying a word which might awaken your suspicion. You told me again that all this had been providential for our love.

"I fell in love with you at once, as soon as I set eyes on you. We had prayed a lot at Lourdes before we went to Luchon. I realised when I met you that our prayers were answered."

You had no glimmering of the irritation that these words aroused in me. Your adversaries, secretly, have a much higher idea of religion than you imagine, or than they believe themselves. Otherwise, why should they be hurt by seeing you debase it? Or does it really seem quite simple in your eyes to ask even temporal blessings from that God Whom you call Father? . . .

But what does all that matter? It emerged from what you said that your family and yourself had swooped hungrily upon the first snail you saw.

How unequal a match ours was had never entered my head until that moment. It was only because your mother got a crazy idea and conveyed it to your father and yourself. . . .

You told me that the Philipots had threatened to disown you if you married me. Yes, at Luchon, while we were laughing at that idiot, he was doing all he could to persuade the Fondaudèges to break off the match.

"But I stuck to you, my dear; he took all that trouble for nothing."

You told me over and over again that certainly you had nothing to regret. I let you go on talking. I saved my breath. You would not have been so happy, you assured me, with that Rodolphe of yours. He was too good-looking, he didn't really love anybody but himself, he let people fall in love

45

with him. Anybody might have taken him away from you.

You did not realise that your very voice changed when you spoke his name. It was softer, with a kind of tremor, a kind of cooing, as though old sighs were held in suspense within your breast, which the mere name of Rodolphe released.

He would not have made you happy, because he was handsome, charming, beloved. That meant that I gave you joy, thanks to my thankless face, my surly manner which put people off. He was one of those unbearable kind of fellows who had been to Cambridge and aped English ways. . . . Would you really have had a husband incapable of choosing the stuff for a suit, or knotting a tie, who hated sports, and did not practise that clever frivolity, that art of eluding serious subjects, that science of living happily and gracefully?

No, you had taken him, this poor fellow, because you had found him there, that year when your mother, suffering from her climacteric, had persuaded herself that you were not "marriageable"; because you neither would nor could stay unmarried six months longer; because he had enough money to provide an adequate excuse in the eyes of the world. . . .

I suppressed my quick breathing, I clenched my fists, I bit my lower lip. When it happens to me to-day I feel such a horror of myself that I cannot stand myself, mind or body, my thoughts go back to that youth of 1885, that husband of twenty-three, with his two arms pressed against his breast, desperately stifling his young love.

I shivered. You noticed it and broke off.

"Are you cold, Louis?"

I replied that it was only a shudder. It was nothing.

"You're not jealous, surely? That would be too silly. . . ."

I was not lying when I assured you that there was not a trace of jealousy in me. How could you have understood that the tragedy was being played out beyond all jealousy?

Far as you were from realising how deeply wounded I

was, still you were upset by my silence. Your hand groped for my face in the darkness and stroked it. There was no dampness of tears upon it; but perhaps that hand of yours did not recognise the familiar features in that set face, with its clenched teeth. You were afraid. To light the candle, you leant half across me. You could not reach the matches. I stifled under the weight of your hateful body.

"What's the matter with you? Don't lie there saying nothing. You're frightening me."

I pretended to be surprised. I assured you that there was nothing wrong with me to be frightened about.

"How stupid of you, my dear, to frighten me like that! I'll put the light out again. I'm going to sleep."

You had nothing more to say. I watched the birth of the new day, that day of my new life. The swallows twittered in the eaves. A man crossed the courtyard, dragging his clogs.

All that I can still hear forty-five years later I heard then: the cocks, the chimes, a goods train on the viaduct; and all that I breathed then I still breathe: that scent I love, that scent of ashes in the wind when there has been a forest fire in the Landes towards the sea.

Suddenly I half sat up.

"Isa, that night when you cried, that evening when we were sitting on that bench, on the Superbagnères path— was it because of him?"

You made no reply, and I seized your arm. You wrenched it away, with a snarl almost like an animal. You turned on your side. You were asleep, with your long hair all about you. Nipped by the cool of dawn, you had pulled the bedclothes anyhow over your huddled body, curled up as young animals sleep.

What was the good of disturbing you out of that child's repose? What I wanted to hear from your lips—did I not know it already?

I got up without making a sound, went barefoot to the

glass in the wardrobe, and looked at myself, as though I were another man, or rather as though I had become my-self again: the man whom nobody had ever loved, for whom nobody in the world had ever suffered. I mourned for my youth. My big peasant's hand stroked my unshaven cheek, already dark with hard bristles, red where the light caught them.

I dressed in silence and went down to the garden. Mamma was in the rose-walk. She used to get up before the servants to air the house.

"Making the best of the cool, are you?" she said to me; and she pointed to the mist that covered the plain. "It will be scorching to-day. At eight o'clock I'll shut up every-thing."

I kissed her more lovingly than usual. She whispered: "My dear . . ."

My heart (does it astonish you that I speak of my heart?), my heart was nearly bursting. Hesitating words came to my lips. . . . Where was I to begin? Would she understand? There is an ease about silence to which I al-ways succumb.

I went down to the terrace. Thin fruit-trees stood out vaguely above the vines. A spur of the hills raised the mist and parted it. A tower was born from it; then the church emerged from it in turn, like a living body.

You who imagine that I have never understood any of these things. . . . I felt, nevertheless, at that moment, that a human being, broken as I was, may seek the reason, the meaning, of his undoing; that it is possible that this undoing has a significance; that events, especially those that touch the heart, are perhaps messengers whose secret has to be interpreted. . . . Yes, I was capable, at certain hours of my life, of glimpsing things that might have drawn me closer to you.

In any case, that morning, it cannot have been a feeling of more than a few seconds. I can still see myself going back to the house. It was not yet eight o'clock, and already the sun was striking hard.

You were at your window, with your head bent, holding your hair in one hand and brushing it with the other. You did not see me. I stood for a moment with my head raised towards you, in prey to a hatred of which I can still feel the bitter taste in my mouth, after all these years.

I hastened to my desk. I opened a locked drawer. I took out of it a little, crumpled handkerchief, the same that had served to dry your tears, that evening at Superbagnères, and that I, poor fool, had pressed against my heart. I took it; I tied a stone to it, as I might have done to a living dog that I wanted to drown; and I threw it into that pond which, in our dialect, has a name that sounds like "gutter."

Chapter V

THEN began the era of the great silence which, for forty years past, has scarcely ever been broken. Nothing of this collapse appeared on the outside. Everything went on as it had done in the days when I was happy.

We remained nevertheless united in the flesh; but the phantom of Rodolphe was no longer born of our embrace, and you never mentioned that fearful name again. He had come at your summons, he had hovered over our bed, he had accomplished his work of destruction. Now he could afford to keep quiet and await the long sequence of effects, the chain of consequences.

Perhaps you felt that you had been wrong to speak. You had no idea that it mattered very much; you simply thought that it was wiser to banish that name from our conversation. I do not know whether you noticed that we no longer talked as we used to do, at night. There was an end to our endless talks. We never said anything again without thinking about it first. Each of us was on guard.

I used to waken in the middle of the night; I used to be awakened by my suffering. I was linked to you like the fox to the trap. I imagined the conversation we might have if I had shaken you roughly, if I had thrown you out of bed.

"No," you would have cried, "I didn't lie to you, because I was in love with you."

"Yes, as a makeshift, and because it is always easy to use physical attraction, which means nothing, to make the other person believe that one loves him. I am not a monster. The first girl that came along who loved me could have done what she liked with me."

Sometimes I groaned in the darkness; and you did not waken.

Your first pregnancy, moreover, made any explanation idle, and little by little changed the relations between us. It was before the grape-gathering. We went back to town, and you had a miscarriage and had to lie quiet for several weeks. In the spring you became pregnant again. We had to take great care of you.

So began those years of pregnancies, accidents and births that provided me with more pretexts than I needed to draw away from you. I plunged into a life of secret debauchery —very secret, for I was beginning to appear in court a good deal, I was "at my business," as Mamma said, and it was a question for me of being careful of my reputation. I had my hours and my habits. Life in a provincial town develops in the debauchee the wily instinct of hunted game.

Don't be afraid, Isa: I shall spare you what you hold in horror. You need not fear any picture of that hell into which I descended almost every day. You threw me back into it, you who had pulled me out of it.

Even if I had been less prudent, you would have seen nothing but passion in it. From the moment of Hubert's birth you revealed your true nature: you were a mother, nothing but a mother. Your attention was turned away from me. You no longer saw me; it was absolutely true that you had no eyes except for the children. By giving you them I had accomplished all that you expected of me.

So long as the children were small and I took no interest in them, no conflict could arise between us. We met only in those ritual performances in which bodies act by force of habit—in which a man and a woman are both thousands of miles away from their own flesh.

You did not begin to perceive that I existed until I, in my turn, began to hover round these little ones. You did not begin to hate me until I claimed to have rights over them. Rejoice over the confession which I dare to make to you: paternal instinct did not impel me. Very soon I became jealous of that passion which they had awakened in you. Yes, I wanted to take them from you in order to punish you. I gave myself high-minded reasons; I put forward the demands of duty. I did not want a bigoted woman to warp the minds of my children. But that's what it really was!

Shall I ever get to the end of this story? I began it for you; and already it seems unlikely that you will go on following me. Fundamentally, it is for myself that I am writing. Old lawyer that I am, I put my case in order; I assemble the evidence of my life—of this case that I lost.

Those chimes. . . . To-morrow, Easter. I shall come down in honour of this holy day, I promise you. "The children are complaining that they never see you," you told me this morning. Our daughter Geneviève was with you, standing beside my bed. You went out and left us alone together: she had something to ask me. I had heard you whispering in the passage. "It would be better if you spoke first," you told Geneviève. . . .

It was about her son-in-law, of course, that blackguard Phili. How clever I was in changing the conversation, in order to prevent the question from being put! Geneviève went away without having been able to say anything to me. I know what she wanted. I overheard it all, the other day. When the drawing-room window is open, underneath mine, I have only to lean out a little.

It is a question of advancing the capital that Phili needs to buy a share in a stockbroking firm. An investment just like any other, of course. . . . As though I had not seen the storm blowing up; as though it were not a matter now of putting one's money under lock and key! . . . If only they knew how much I have made, this last month, because I sensed a slump in stocks! . . .

They have all gone to Vespers. Easter has emptied the house and the fields. I am left alone, an old Faust cut off from the joy of life by cruel old age. They do not know what old age is.

At lunch they were all ears to catch what fell from my lips about the Stock Exchange and business. I was talking especially for the benefit of Hubert, so that he should pull up, if he has time. How anxiously he listened to me. . . . There's a man who cannot hide the game he's playing!

He emptied the plate you piled up for him, with that obstinacy of poor mothers who see their children devoured by anxiety and still make them eat, as though that were so much to the good, so much saved out of the wreck! And he snapped at you, as I used to snap at my mother.

And the care with which young Phili kept my glass filled; and the pretended solicitude of his wife, little Janine! "Grandfather, you shouldn't smoke. Even one cigarette is too much for you. Are you sure that they haven't made a mistake, that this coffee is really de-caffeined?" She plays her game badly, poor girl, she rings false. Her voice, the way she speaks, give her away entirely. You too, when you were a young woman, used to be affected. But from the time of your first pregnancy you became yourself again.

Janine, for her part, to the day of her death will be a lady who keeps herself abreast of the times, repeats whatever she hears that strikes her as distinctive, borrows opinions about everything and understands nothing about anything. How can Phili, so earthy, a gay dog of a fellow, stand living with that little idiot? No, I'm wrong! Everything is false about her, except her passion for him. She plays her part so badly just because nothing counts in her eyes, nothing exists, except her love.

After lunch we all sat on the steps. Janine and Phili looked at Geneviève, Janine's mother, with a beseeching air; and she in her turn looked at you. You made an almost imperceptible sign of refusal. Then Geneviève got up and asked me:

"Papa, would you like to come for a walk with me?"

How afraid you all are of me! I took pity on her.

Though I had originally made up my mind not to stir, I got up and took her arm. We walked round the meadow. The family watched us from the steps. She went to the heart of the matter at once.

"I wanted to talk to you about Phili."

She was trembling. It is a frightful thing to make one's children afraid. But do you suppose that one is free, at sixty-eight, to have anything but an implacable air about him? At that age the expression of the features no longer changes; and the soul is discouraged when it cannot express itself externally. . . .

Geneviève got what she had ready to say off her mind quickly. It was, in fact, a question of a share in a brokerage firm. She insisted upon the very point best calculated to turn me against her. According to her, the fact that Phili had nothing to do was compromising the future of Janine's wedded life with him. Phili was beginning to stray.

I told Geneviève that, in the case of a fellow like her son-in-law, his "share in a stockbroker's" would never serve to supply him with alibis. She defended him. Everybody loves him, this Phili of ours. "You mustn't be harder on him than Janine is. . . ." I protested that I neither judged nor condemned him. The gentleman's amorous career did not interest me in the least.

"Does he take any interest in me? Why should I take any interest in him?"

"He admires you tremendously. . . ."

This brazen lie enabled me to get off what I had in reserve.

"That, my dear daughter, doesn't prevent your Phili from calling me 'the old crocodile.' Don't deny it; I've heard him behind my back, many a time. . . . I don't reject the name: crocodile I am, and crocodile I shall remain. There is nothing to expect from an old crocodile, nothing—except his death. And even dead"—I was rash enough to add—"even dead, he may still act like one." (How I regret having said that, having given her any ground for suspicion!)

Geneviève was overwhelmed. She offered excuses—as though I attached any importance to the insulting nickname. It is Phili's youth that is hateful to me. How can she conceive what he represents, in the eyes of a hated and despairing old man—this triumphant youth, who has been intoxicated from his adolescence with something that I have not tasted in half a century of life?

I hate, I detest all young people: but him more than anybody else. Like a cat that creeps in silently through the window, he penetrated velvet-footed into my house, lured by the scent. My grand-daughter did not bring him a very good dowry, but she had, by way of compensation, great "expectations." The expectations of our children! To obtain them, they have to pass over our bodies.

While Geneviève was sniffing and dabbing at her eyes, I said to her in an insinuating tone:

"But after all, you have a husband, a husband who deals in rum. Our good Alfred has only to make a position for his son-in-law. Why should I be more generous than you are yourselves?"

She changed her tune to talk to me about poor Alfred. What contempt, what disgust! According to her, he was a spiritless fellow who was reducing his commitments more and more every day. In his business, which used to be so big, there was no room for two left to-day.

I congratulated her on having a husband like that. When the storm is approaching, one must shorten sail. The future was with those who, like Alfred, saw small. To-day lack of big ideas was the first requisite in business. She thought I was making fun of her, though as a matter of fact this is what I most seriously believe—I, who have my money under lock and key, and do not even run the risks of the Savings Bank.

We went back to the house. Geneviève did not dare to say any more. I was not leaning on her arm any longer. The family, sitting in a circle, watched us coming, and no doubt were already in course of interpreting the unfavourable signs. Our return evidently interrupted a discussion between Hubert's family and that of Geneviève's. Oh, what a fine battle there would be about my fortune if I ever agreed to let go of it!

Only Phili was standing up. The wind stirred his rebellious hair. He was wearing a shirt open at the neck, with short sleeves. I have a horror of these youths of to-day, and of our athletic girls. His infantile cheeks turned purple when, in reply to Janine's silly question: "Well, did you have a nice talk?" I answered gently: "We talked about an old crocodile. . . ."

Once more, it is not because of this insult that I hate him. People do not know what old age means. You cannot imagine such a torture as this: to have had nothing out of life, and to await nothing but death—and to feel that there may be nothing beyond this world, that no explanation exists, that the word of the enigma will never be given us. . . .

But you—you have not suffered what I have suffered, and you will never suffer what I am suffering now. The children do not look forward to your death. They love you in their own way; they are fond of you.

It was all at once that they took your side. I used to love them. Geneviève, that fat woman of forty who has just tried to extract four hundred thousand-franc notes out of me for her blackguard of a son-in-law—I remember her as a little girl on my knee. As soon as you saw her in my arms, you called her away. . . .

But I shall never get to the end of this confession if I go on mixing up past and present like this. I must try and introduce a little order into it.

Chapter VI

I do not think that I hated you from the very first year that followed the disastrous night. My hatred was born, little by little, in proportion as I better appreciated how indifferent you were towards me, and that nothing existed in your eyes apart from those wailing, bawling, greedy little beings.

You did not even notice that, at the age of less than thirty, I had become a civil law barrister with more work than he could do, already hailed as a young master at this Bar, the most distinguished in France after that of Paris. Beginning with the Villenave case (1893), I also revealed myself as a great criminal lawyer (it is very rare to excel in both branches), and you were the only person deaf to the universal echo of my pleading. That was also the year in which our misunderstanding became open hostility.

That famous Villenave case, if it set the seal upon my triumph, also tightened the vice which stifled me. Perhaps I still had some hope left. It brought me the proof that I did not exist in your eyes.

Those Villenaves—do you even remember their story?—after forty years of married life, loved one another with a love which had passed into a proverb. People said: "united like the Villenaves." They lived with an only son, aged about fifteen, in their château of Ornon, just outside the town, entertaining very little, sufficient to one another. "A love such as one reads about in books," your mother used to say, in one of those ready-made phrases of which her grand-daughter Geneviève inherited the secret.

I would swear that you have forgotten all about the drama. If I tell it to you, you will jeer at me, as you used to do when, at table, I recalled my examinations . . . but that can't be helped!

One morning, the servant who was doing the downstairs rooms heard a revolver shot on the first floor, a cry of pain. He dashed upstairs. The door of his master's and mistress's room was locked. He overheard low voices, confused sounds of things being moved, hasty steps in the lavatory. After a moment or two, while he was still rattling the handle, the door opened. Villenave was lying on the bed, in his nightshirt, covered with blood. Madame de Villenave, with her hair down, wearing a dressing-gown, was standing at the foot of the bed, with a revolver in her hand. She said: "I have wounded Monsieur de Villenave. Hurry up and get the doctor, the surgeon, and the police superintendent. I won't move from here."

They could get nothing out of her but that confession: "I have wounded my husband," which was confirmed by Monsieur de Villenave, as soon as he was in a condition to speak. He also refused to give any further information.

The accused declined to choose an advocate. As the son-in-law of a friend of theirs, I was entrusted with her defence; but, in my daily visits to the prison, I could get nothing out of that obstinate woman. The most ridiculous stories circulated round the town about her. For my part, from the very first day I had no doubt about her innocence. Yet she charged herself, and the husband who loved her permitted her to charge herself. Oh, the *flair* of men who are not loved for getting on the track of passion in others!

That woman was entirely possessed by conjugal love. She had not fired at her husband. Had she made a rampart of his body by mistake, in the effort to defend him against some rejected lover? Nobody had entered the house since the night before. There was nobody who was in the habit of visiting them . . . well, I need not go over the whole of that old story for you.

Until the morning of the day when I had to plead, I had decided to confine myself to a negative attitude and to show simply that Madame de Villenave could not have committed the crime of which she was accused. It was, at the last moment, the testimony of young Yves, her son, or rather—for his testimony in itself was of no importance and threw no light—the beseeching and imperious way in which his mother kept looking at him until he had left the witness-stand, and the kind of relief which she revealed then, that suddenly rent the veil for me.

I denounced the son, that sickly adolescent, jealous of his too much loved father. I threw myself, with impassioned logic, into that now famous improvisation, in which Professor F., on his own admission, found the essential germ of his system, and which transformed both the study of the psychology of adolescence and the therapeutics of its neuroses.

If I recall this memory, my dear Isa, it is not because I cherish the hope of arousing, forty years afterwards, an admiration which you never felt at the moment of my triumph, when the newspapers of two hemispheres were publishing my picture. But at the same time as your indifference, at that crucial moment in my career, gave me the measure of my loneliness and my solitude, I had also had under my eyes for weeks, I had had inside the four walls of a cell, that woman who sacrificed herself, not so much to save her own child as to save the son of her husband, the heir to his name.

It was he, the victim, who had implored her: "Accuse yourself. . . ." She had carried love to the point of making the world believe that she was a criminal, that she had tried to kill the only man she had ever loved. Conjugal love, not maternal love, had impelled her. . . . (The sequel showed that clearly: she separated from her son, and on one pretext or another always lived apart from him.)

I might have been a man loved as Villenave was. I saw a good deal of him, too, at the time of the case. What did he possess more than I? He was handsome enough, and well born, no doubt; but he cannot have had much brains.

His hostile attitude to me after the trial showed that. And I had a kind of genius. If I had had, at that moment, a wife who loved me, to what heights might I not have risen?

One cannot preserve one's faith in himself all alone. We must have a witness of our prowess: somebody who notes the hits, who counts the points, who crowns us on the day of rewards—just as before, on prize-day, when I was loaded down with books, my eyes searched for my mother in the crowd, and, to the sound of military music, she laid the golden laurels on my freshly cropped head.

At the time of the Villenave case, she was beginning to fail. I only realised it little by little. The interest which she took in a little black dog, that barked furiously whenever I approached, was the first sign of her decline. Every time I went to see her she talked about nothing but this animal. She ceased to listen to what I said about myself.

In any case, she could not have filled the place of the love that would have saved me, at this turning-point in my life. Her vice, which was being too fond of money, she had bequeathed to me. I had that passion in my blood. She would have bent all her efforts towards keeping me in a profession in which, as she said, I "made big money." At a time when literature attracted me, when I was in demand by the newspapers and all the leading reviews, when during the elections the groups of the Left offered me the candidature for La Bastide (the man who accepted instead of me was elected with ease), I resisted the call of ambition because I did not want to give up "big money."

That was your desire too, and you gave me to understand that you would never leave the provinces. A wife who loved me would have been proud of my fame. She would have taught me that the art of living consists in sacrificing a lower passion to a higher passion. The idiots of journalists, who pretend to be indignant because such-and-such an advocate profits by the fact that he is a deputy or a minister to glean some small pickings, would do better to admire the conduct of those who have succeeded in establishing an intelligent hierarchy among their passions, and preferred political fame to more profitable business.

The defect of which you could have cured me, if you had loved me, was that of putting nothing higher than immediate gain, of being incapable of letting the petty, mediocre prey of fat fees go for the shadow of power; for there is no shadow without reality; the shadow is itself a reality. Well, I had nothing but the consolation of "making big money," like the corner grocer.

Such is what remains to me: that is what I have gained, in the course of these dreadful years, this money which you are mad enough to think that I might relinquish. Why, the very idea that you should enjoy it after my death is unbearable to me! I told you at the beginning that originally I had made such dispositions that you would not get any of it. I have given you to understand that I have forgone this revenge. . . .

But, when I said this, I misunderstood the movement, like that of the tide, of hatred in my heart. Sometimes it ebbs, and I soften. . . . Then it flows, and its miry waves swallow me up again.

From to-day, from this Easter Day, after that attempt to despoil me to the profit of your Phili, and since I have seen, as a whole, that family pack sitting in a circle before the door and watching me, I am obsessed by the vision of a sharing-up of the spoils—of a sharing-up which will set you at one another's throats; for you will fight like dogs over my land, over my securities.

The land will be yours; but the securities no longer exist. Those which I mentioned to you, on the first page of this letter, I sold last week, at the highest possible price. Since then they have gone down every day. All ships founder, as soon as I abandon them; I never make a mistake.

My liquid millions, you shall have them too—you shall have them if I choose. There are days when I make up my mind that you shall not lay hands on a single halfpenny of them. . . .

I hear your gang whispering as you all come upstairs. You have stopped; you are talking without fear of my being awake (it is understood that I am deaf); I can see the light of your candles under the door. I recognise Phili's falsetto (one would think that he was still moulting), and now I hear stifled laughter, the cackling of young women. You are scolding them; you are just going to tell them: "I assure you he isn't asleep. . . ."

You are coming to my door; you are listening; you are looking through the key-hole—my lamp gives me away. You are going back to the pack; you must be whispering to them: "He's still awake, he's listening to you. . . ."

They are stealing away on tip-toe. The steps of the staircase are creaking. Doors are shutting one by one. This Easter night, the house is full of couples.

And I—I might be the living trunk of these young branches. Most fathers are loved. But you were my enemy, and my children have gone over to the enemy.

It is with this war that I must deal now. I have no strength to write any more. But still I hate going to bed, lying down, even when the state of my heart lets me. At my age, sleep attracts the attention of death; one must not look as though he were dead. So long as I am sitting up, it seems to me as though death cannot come.

What do I fear from it? Is it physical pain, the pain of the last sigh? No; what I fear is rather that it is something which does not exist, which can only be expressed by the symbol – .

Chapter VII

SO long as our three little ones remained in the limbo of early childhood, our enmity remained masked. The atmosphere of our home weighed heavily. Your indifference towards me, your detachment from everything that concerned me, prevented you from being affected by it, or even feeling it.

As for me, I was seldom in it. I lunched alone at eleven o'clock, in time to get to the Law Courts before noon. My cases took up most of my time, and what little I might have had to spend at home—you can guess how I spent it.

Why this frightful sheer debauchery, lacking in anything which, as a rule, serves as an excuse; reduced to its mere horror, without a shadow of sentiment, without the least pretence of affection? I might easily have had those kinds of adventure which the world applauds. How could a barrister of my age avoid certain temptations? Plenty of women wanted to get beyond the advocate and intrigue the man. . . .

But I had lost faith in the creatures, or rather in my power to attract any of them. At first sight, I detected self-interest animating those who showed themselves complaisant, who beckoned to me. The preconceived idea that they were all trying to make money out of me froze me. Why should I not admit that, to the tragic certitude that I was a man whom nobody could love, there was added the distrust of the rich man who is afraid of being duped, who suspects that he is being exploited?

As for you, I had "pensioned you off." You knew me too well to expect a halfpenny more from me than the agreed sum. It was a good round sum, and you never exceeded it. I never felt any danger in that direction.

But other women! I was one of those fools who persuade themselves that there are, on the one hand, women who love disinterestedly, and, on the other hand, adventuresses who are only out for money. As though, in the case of most women, amorous inclination did not go hand in hand with a need to be maintained, protected, spoilt! . . .

At the age of sixty-eight, I realise, with a clearness which sometimes makes me want to howl, all that I repelled, not through virtue, but through distrust and cowardice. The few liaisons which I attempted came to an early end, either because my suspicious mind interpreted the most innocent requests wrongly, or as a result of those ways of mine with which you are only too familiar: those arguments over restaurant bills, or with drivers about tips.

I like to know in advance what I have to pay. I like everything to have its tariff. Dare I confess this shameful thing? What I liked about debauchery, perhaps, was that it had its fixed price.

But, in the case of a man like myself, what link could there be between the heart's desire and mere desire? Heart's desires—I did not believe any longer that they could ever be satisfied; I strangled them at birth. I was a past-master in the art of killing all sentiment, at that precise moment when the will plays a decisive part in love, when, on the verge of passion, we still remain free to let ourselves go or restrain ourselves.

I went for the simplest thing—what could be obtained for an agreed price. I don't like being "done"; but what I owe, I pay. You complain about my avarice. It does not prevent me from being unable to bear having debts. I pay cash for everything. My tradesmen know it and bless me for it. The idea of owing the smallest sum is unendurable to me. It was in that way that I understood "love": paying cash down, paying cash down. . . . How disgusting!

No, I am making too much of the thing. I am dirtying

myself. I have loved, and perhaps I have been loved. . . .
In 1909, when my youth was waning. What is the use of
passing over this adventure in silence? You knew about it;
you were capable of remembering it when you wanted to
break with me.

I saved that little governess from the reformatory—she
had been prosecuted for infanticide. She gave herself to me
at the beginning out of gratitude; but afterwards . . . Yes,
I found love that year. It was my insatiability that ruined
everything. It was not enough that I should maintain her
in embarrassed circumstances, almost in poverty; she must
be always at my disposal, never see anybody else, so that
I might take her, leave her, pick her up again, as my fancy
dictated during my scanty leisure.

She was my chattel. My taste for possessing, using and
abusing, extends to human beings. I ought to have had
slaves. Just once, I thought I had found a victim, made to
the measure of my demands. I watched even over her
glances. . . . But I am forgetting my promise not to entertain you with such matters. She went off to Paris; she could
not stand it any longer.

"If it was only we with whom you couldn't get on," you
have often told me; "but everybody else as well distrusts
and shuns you, Louis, you must see that for yourself. . . ."
Yes, I saw it. . . . At the Law Courts, I was always a soli-
tary. They elected me to the Bar Council as late as possible.
After all the fools that they put before me, I lost any desire
to be President.

For that matter, did I ever want to be? It would have
meant being a delegate, entertaining. Those are honours
that cost dearly; the game is not worth the candle. You—
you wanted it because of the children. Never did you desire
anything for me on my own account. "Do it for the children's sake."

The year that followed our marriage, your father had his
first attack, and the château of Cenon was closed to us.

Very quickly you adopted Calèse. Of me, the only thing that you really accepted was my own countryside. You took root in my soil, without our roots ever being able to meet.

In this house, in this garden, your children spent all their holidays. Our little Marie died here; and, far from her death giving you a horror of it, you attach to the room in which she suffered a sacred character. It was here that you hatched your brood, that you nursed the sick, watched over cradles, had "crows to pluck" with nurses and governesses. It was between these apple-trees that lines were fixed to hang out Marie's little dresses, all that unashamed washing of hers. It was in this drawing-room that Abbé Ardouin assembled the children round the piano and made them sing choruses which, to avert my anger, were not always canticles.

Smoking in front of the house, on summer evenings, I used to listen to their pure voices: that air of Lulli's, *Ah, these woods, these rocks, these fountains.* . . . It was a quiet happiness from which I knew myself to be excluded, a zone of purity and dreaming which was forbidden to me: tranquil love, a drowsy wave that came and died a few yards away from my rock.

I went into the drawing-room, and the voices fell silent. All conversation ceased at my approach. Geneviève buried herself in a book. Only Marie was not afraid of me; I called her and she came; I took her in my arms forcibly, but she nestled there readily enough. I could feel her little bird's heart beating. As soon as I let her go, she flew out into the garden . . . Marie!

Very early the children were troubled about my absence from Mass and my Friday cutlet. But the struggle between the two of us, under their eyes, witnessed only a small number of violent outbursts, in which I was generally beaten. After every such defeat, a subterranean warfare continued. Calèse was the theatre of it, for in town I was never at home. But the legal vacation coincided with the school holidays, and August and September assembled us here.

I remember that day when we collided head-on—in connection with a joke which I had made before Geneviève, who was reciting her Sacred History. I asserted my right to defend my children's minds, and you opposed to me the duty of protecting their souls. I had been beaten once already, by consenting to Hubert being entrusted to the Jesuit Fathers, and the little girls to the nuns of the Sacred Heart. I had bowed to the prestige which the traditions of the Fondaudège family always retained in my eyes.

But I thirsted for revenge; and besides, what was of importance to me, that day, was that I had put my finger on the one subject which was capable of exasperating you, on the one that drove you to emerge from your indifference and give me your attention—even the attention of hate. I had at last found a meeting-place. At last I could force you to come to grips with me.

Hitherto irreligion had been for me merely an empty form, into which I had poured my humiliations as an enriched little peasant, despised by his middle-class comrades. Now I filled it with my disappointment in love and with an almost infinite resentment.

The dispute flared up again during lunch. I asked you what pleasure the Eternal Being could take in seeing you eat salmon-trout rather than stewed beef. You left the table. I remember how the children stared. I followed you to your room. Your eyes were dry. You spoke to me with the utmost possible calmness.

I realised, that day, that you had taken more notice of my way of life than I had thought. You had laid hands on some letters: material for obtaining a separation. "I have stayed with you because of the children. But if your presence is to be a danger to their souls, I shall not hesitate."

No, you would not have hesitated to leave me—me and my money. Selfish as you were, there was no sacrifice which you would not have accepted in order that, in those little

ones, there should remain intact the deposit of Dogma, that
assembly of habits, of formulæ—that stupidity.

I have not kept the insulting letter which you wrote me
after the death of Marie. You had the whip hand. My position would have been dangerously shaken by a separation
suit between us: at that period, and in the provinces, people did not treat the subject as a joke. Rumour already had
it that I was a Freemason; my ideas put me on the border-
line of society; and, but for the prestige of your family, they
might have done me the greatest injury.

And above all—in case of separation, I should have had
to return the Suez Canal shares of your dowry. I had grown
used to regarding these securities as my own. The idea of
having to surrender them was horrible to me—not to speak
of the income which your father allowed us. . . .

I pocketed my pride, and gave in to all your demands;
but I decided to devote my leisure to winning over the children. I took this decision in August, 1896. Those sad, hot
summers of long ago merge in my mind, and the memories
that I recall here extend over about five years, 1895 to 1900.

I did not think that it would be difficult to take the children in hand again. I counted on the prestige of the father
of the family, and on my brains. A boy of ten, two little
girls—it would only be a game, I thought, to win them over
to me.

I remember their surprise and their anxiety, the day when
I suggested that they should come for a long walk with
Papa. You were sitting in the courtyard, under the silver
lime-tree. They questioned you with their eyes.

"Why, my dears, you needn't ask permission from me!"

We set out. How does one talk to children? I, who am
accustomed to stand up to the Public Prosecutor, or to defending counsel when I plead for the injured party, or to a
whole hostile audience; I, whom the presiding judge at As-
sizes respects—I am intimidated by children: by children,
and also by lower-class people, even those peasants whose

son I am. In their presence I am unsure of my ground, tongue-tied.

The little ones were nice to me, but on their guard. You had occupied these three hearts beforehand; you held all the ways into them. It was impossible to advance there without your permission. Too scrupulous though you were to demean me in their eyes, you had not concealed the fact that they must pray a lot for "poor Papa." Whatever I did, I had my fixed place in their scheme of things: I was poor Papa, who had to be prayed for a lot, and whose conversion had to be obtained. Everything that I might say or hint about religion only confirmed the simple image which they made of me.

They lived in a miraculous world, festooned with festivals piously celebrated. You could get them to do what you liked by talking to them about the first Communion which they had just made or for which they were preparing. When they sang, in the evening, on the steps of Calèse, it was not always Lulli's airs to which I had to listen, but also psalms. I could see the amorphous group of you in the distance, and, when there was moonlight, I could make out three little figures standing up. My steps on the gravel interrupted the singing.

Every Sunday the bustle of departure for Mass awakened me. You were always afraid of being late. The horses snorted. Somebody called the cook, who was behind time. One of the children had forgotten his prayer-book. A shrill voice cried: "What Sunday after Pentecost is it?"

On their return they came to kiss me "Good morning," and found me still in bed. Little Marie, who had doubtless recited all the prayers she had been taught for my benefit, looked at me fixedly, in the hope, presumably, of seeing some slight improvement in my spiritual condition.

She alone did not irritate me. Whereas the two elder children were already established in the beliefs which you professed, together with that middle-class instinct for comfort which was later to make them set aside all the heroic

69

virtues, there was in Marie, on the contrary, a touching fervour, a tenderness of heart for the servants, for the farm-labourers, for the poor. People said of her: "She would give away everything she has; money does not stick to her fingers. She's very pretty, but she will want watching. . . ." They also said: "Nobody can resist her, not even her father."

She came and sat on my knee of her own accord in the evening. Once she went to sleep against my shoulder. Her curls tickled my face. I felt cramped, and I wanted to smoke; but I did not stir. When her nurse came for her, at nine o'clock, I carried her up to her room myself, and you looked at me in amazement, as though I were that wild beast that licked the feet of little martyrs. A few days afterwards, on the morning of August 14, Marie said to me (you know how children do):

"Promise me to do what I'm going to ask you. . . . Promise first, and I'll tell you afterwards. . . ."

She reminded me that you were singing at eleven o'clock Mass next day, and told me that it would be nice if I came and listened to you.

"You've promised! You've promised!" she kept on saying as she kissed me. "You've given your word!"

She took the kiss which I gave her in return for acquiescence. The whole household was told about it. I felt myself under observation. Monsieur was going to Mass to-morrow —he who never set foot in a church! It was an event of immense significance.

I sat down to table, that evening, in a state of irritation which I could not hide for long. Hubert asked you some question or other about the Dreyfus affair. I remember that I protested furiously against what you told him in reply. I left the table and did not return. I packed a bag, and, at dawn on August 15, I caught the six o'clock train and spent a frightful day in a stifling, deserted Bordeaux.

It was strange that after that you should ever have seen me at Calèse again. Why did I always spend my holidays with all of you instead of travelling? I might invent all sorts of fine reasons. To tell the truth, it was a question for me of avoiding doubled expense. It never occurred to me that it was possible to go away and spend a lot of money without, as a preliminary, draining the stock-pot and shutting up the house.

I could have taken no pleasure in travelling about, knowing all the time that I was leaving the usual household routine behind me. So long as my share was served at Calèse, why should I go and eat elsewhere? Such was the spirit of economy that my mother had bequeathed to me, and out of which I made a virtue.

So I went back, but in a state of resentment against which even Marie herself was powerless. I started new tactics against you. Far from attacking your beliefs directly, I set myself, on the smallest possible occasion, to put you in contradiction with your faith.

My poor Isa, good Christian though you may be, confess that I had an easy game of it. That charity is synonymous with love was something that you had forgotten, if you ever knew it. Under this name you comprised a certain number of duties towards the poor, which you performed conscientiously, in the interests of your eternal life. I admit that you have changed a great deal in this respect: nowadays you visit cancer cases, I grant you.

But at that time, once the poor—your poor—were relieved, you found yourself only the more at your ease to demand your due from the people who lived dependent upon you. You never compromised about the duty of a housewife, which is to obtain the utmost possible work for the least possible money. That poor old woman who came in the morning with her vegetable cart, and to whom you would have dispensed charity freely if she had been a beggar, never sold you a single head of salad without your making it a point of honour to beat her down a halfpenny or so on her modest profits.

The most timid requests of the servants and the labourers

for any increase in wages aroused in you at first stunned surprise, and then an indignation whose vehemence gave you the upper hand and always assured you the last word. You had a kind of genius for showing these people that they lacked for nothing. In your mouth an endless enumeration multiplied the advantages which they enjoyed. "You have lodging, a cask of wine, half a pig which you feed on my potatoes, a garden in which to grow vegetables." The poor devils had no idea how well off they were.

You declared that your housemaid could put the whole of the forty francs a month you paid her in the Savings Bank. "She has all my old dresses, all my petticoats, all my shoes. What does she want money for? She would only give it away to her family. . . ."

It is true that you looked after them devotedly when they were ill; you never neglected them; and I recognise that in general you were always esteemed, and often even loved, by these people, who despise weak masters. About all these questions you professed the ideas of your environment and your time.

But you would never admit to yourself that the Gospel condemned these ideas. "By the way," I used to say, "I believe that Christ said . . ." You stopped short, disconcerted, furious because of the children. You always ended by falling into the trap. "One must not take things literally . . ." you would stammer. Whereupon I triumphed with ease, and overwhelmed you with examples to prove to you that saintliness consisted precisely in following the Gospel literally. If you had the misfortune to protest that you were not a saint, I quoted you the precept: "Be ye perfect, as your Heavenly Father is perfect."

Confess, my poor Isa, that I did you good in my own way, and that, if you visit the cancerous to-day, they owe it partly to me! At that time your love for the children monopolised you altogether; they ate up your reserves of kindness and self-sacrifice. They prevented you from seeing other people. It was not only from me that they had turned you away, but from the rest of the world as well.

To God Himself you could speak only about their health and their future. That was where I had my chance. I used to ask you whether, from the Christian point of view, one should not rather desire all kinds of crosses for them, poverty, sickness. You cut me short. "I won't answer you; you are talking about things you don't understand."

But, unfortunately for you, the children's tutor was there too, a seminarist of twenty-three, Abbé Ardouin, whose testimony I mercilessly invoked and whom I embarrassed very much; for I never made him intervene except when I was sure that I was right, and he was incapable, in debates of that kind, of saying anything but just what he thought. In proportion as the Dreyfus affair developed, I found opportunities by the thousand of setting the poor abbé against you.

"To disorganise the army for the sake of a wretched Jew . . ." you would say. The mere word was enough to arouse my pretended indignation, and I kept on until I drove Abbé Ardouin to admit that a Christian could not subscribe to the condemnation of an innocent man, even if the safety of the country were at stake.

I did not really try to convince you, you and the children, who knew nothing about "the Affair" except through the caricatures of "right-thinking" newspapers. You formed an untouchable whole. Even when I appeared to be right, you were quite sure that it was only by some trickery or other.

You reached the point of saying nothing in my presence. At my approach, as happened again to-day, discussion came to a dead stop. But sometimes you did not know that I was hiding behind a clump of bushes, and suddenly I intervened before you could beat a retreat, and you were compelled to accept battle.

"He is a saint of a boy," you used to say about Abbé Ardouin, "but a regular child who never thinks evil. My husband plays with him like a cat with a mouse. That's the only reason he tolerates him, in spite of his horror of cassocks."

As a matter of fact, I had agreed to the presence of an ecclesiastical tutor in the first place because no lay tutor would have accepted a hundred and fifty francs for the whole period of the holidays. At the outset I took this tall, dark, short-sighted young man, crippled by shyness, for a person of no importance, and paid no more attention to him than if he were a piece of furniture.

He made the children work, took them for walks, ate very little, and never said a word. He went up to his room as soon as he had swallowed his last mouthful. Sometimes, when there was nobody in the house, he sat down at the piano. I know nothing about music, but, as you used to say, "he gave me pleasure."

No doubt you have not forgotten an incident which, without your ever suspecting it, created a hidden current of attraction between Abbé Ardouin and myself. One day the children announced that the priest was coming. Immediately, as was my custom, I took flight in the direction of the vineyard. But you sent Hubert after me: the priest had an urgent communication to make to me. I went back to the house cursing and swearing; for I was very much in awe of that little old man.

He had come, he told me, to unburden his conscience. He had recommended Abbé Ardouin to us as an excellent seminarist, whose subdiaconate had been postponed for reasons of health. He had just learned, however, in the course of an ecclesiastical retreat, that this delay was rather to be attributed to a disciplinary measure. Abbé Ardouin, although very pious, was mad about music, and he had been tempted by one of his comrades to slip out one night and attend a charity concert at the Grand Theatre. Although they were in lay clothes, they were recognised and reported.

What crowned the scandal was that the interpreter of Thais, Mme Georgette Lebrun, figured on the programme.

At her appearance bare-legged, in her Greek tunic, held up under the arms by a silver girdle—"and that was all, so they said, not even the smallest shoulder-strap"—there was an "Oh!" of indignation. From the Union box an old gentleman cried out: "This is a bit too strong. . . . Where are we supposed to be?"

Such was what Abbé Ardouin and his comrade had witnessed! One of the delinquents was expelled on the spot. The other was forgiven; he was a first-rate student; but his superiors had delayed his ordination by two years.

We were agreed in protesting that we had every confidence in the abbé all the same. Henceforth, nevertheless, the priest showed considerable coldness towards the seminarist, who, he said, had deceived him. You may remember this incident; but what you have never known is that that evening, while I was smoking on the terrace, I saw the thin figure of the culprit coming towards me in the moonlight.

He approached me awkwardly, and begged my pardon for having introduced himself into my house without having told me about his scrape. When I assured him that I really liked him all the better for his escapade, he protested with sudden firmness and pleaded against himself.

I could not properly estimate the enormity of his fault, he said; he had sinned at one and the same time against obedience, against his vocation, and against morality. He had committed the sin of scandal. His life would not be long enough to repair what he had done. . . . I can still see that long bent back, with its shadow in the moonlight cut in two by the parapet of the terrace.

Prejudiced though I was against men of his profession, in the presence of such shame and sorrow I could not suspect the least hypocrisy. He excused himself for his silence to us on the ground that he would otherwise have had to go and live for two months at the expense of his mother, a very poor widow who was a daily worker at Libourne. When I answered him that, so far as I could see, he was under no obligation to tell us about an incident which con-

cerned the discipline of the seminary, he took me by the
hand and said these extraordinary words, which I heard for
the first time in my life, and which gave me a kind of
stupor:

"You are very good."

You know that laugh of mine, that laugh which, even
at the beginning of our life together, got on your nerves—
so little infectious that, in my mouth, it had the power of
chilling all gaiety around me. It shook me, that evening,
before that tall seminarist, who was taken aback. Finally I
was able to speak.

"You have no idea, Monsieur l'Abbé, how funny what
you say is. Ask the people who know me whether I am
good. Question my family, my colleagues: badness is my
life force."

He replied, in an embarrassed kind of way, that a really
bad man did not talk about his badness.

"I challenge you," I added, "to find in my life what you
would call a good action."

Then, referring to my profession, he quoted me the words
of Christ: "I was a prisoner, and you visited me. . . ."

"I find it to my advantage, Monsieur l'Abbé. I act from
professional interest. There was a time when I paid warders
to slip my name into the ears of accused persons at a suita-
ble moment. . . . So you see!"

I have forgotten his reply. We walked about under the
lime-trees. How astonished you would have been if I had
told you that I found some comfort in the presence of that
man in a cassock! It was true, though.

I used to get up with the sun and go outside to breathe
the cool air of dawn. I watched the abbé on his way to
Mass, walking fast, so absorbed that he sometimes passed
me a few yards away without seeing me. That was the
time when I overwhelmed you with my mockeries, when
I devoted myself to putting you in contradiction with your
principles. . . . It did not prevent me from having a bad
conscience.

Every time I caught you red-handed in avarice or harshness, I pretended to believe that no trace of the spirit of Christ still survived among any of you; and I was well aware that, under my own roof, a man was living according to that spirit, unknown to all the rest of you.

Chapter VIII

BUT there was one occasion when I had no difficulty in feeling a horror of you. In '96 or '97—you may remember the exact date—our brother-in-law, Baron Philipot, died. Your sister Marinette awakened one morning and spoke to him, and he did not answer. She opened the shutters, saw the turned-up eyes of the old man, his dropped lower jaw, and did not realise all at once that for some hours she had been sleeping side by side with a corpse.

I doubt whether any of you appreciated the horribleness of that wretched man's will. He left his wife an enormous fortune on condition that she did not marry again. If she did, the bulk of it was to go to his nephews.

"We shall have to take the greatest care of her," your mother kept on saying. "Fortunately we are a family that sticks together. We must not leave the little one alone."

Marinette was about thirty at that time; but remember what a girl she looked. She had obediently let herself be married to an old man, and had put up with him without rebelling. You assumed that she could easily accept the obligation to remain a widow. You took no account of the shock of deliverance, that sudden escape from the tunnel into the light of day.

No, Isa, don't be afraid that I am going to abuse the advantage which is given me here. It was natural to desire that those millions should remain in the family and that your children should profit by them. You thought that Marinette ought not to lose the benefit of those ten years of servitude to an old husband. You acted as good relations. Nothing seemed to you more natural than celibacy.

Did you remember yourself that you had once been a

young woman? No, that chapter was finished; you were a mother, and nothing else existed, either for you, or for anybody else. Your family never shone in the way of imagination. You could not put yourselves in the place either of animals or of people.

It was arranged that Marinette should spend the first summer of her widowhood at Calèse. She accepted with delight—not that there was very much intimacy between you; but she loved our children, above all little Marie. As for me, who hardly knew her, what struck me first was her gracefulness. A year older than you, she looked much younger. You let yourself run to seed with the children you bore; she had emerged from that old man's bed apparently intact.

Her face was childlike. She wore her back hair piled high, according to the fashion of that time, and that darkish fair hair of hers strayed over the nape of her neck. (That is a marvel forgotten to-day: a nape with hair on it.) Her rather too round eyes gave her the air of being perpetually surprised. For a joke I joined my two hands round her "wasp's waist"; but the development of her bosom and hips would seem almost monstrous to-day. The women of that time resembled hot-house flowers.

I was surprised that Marinette was so light-hearted. She gave the children plenty of amusement, organised hide-and-seek parties in the loft, played living pictures in the evening. "She is a little too flighty," you said; "she does not realise her position in life."

It was bad enough that you should have to put up with her wearing white dresses during the week; but you struck at her going to Mass without her veil and not wearing a coat trimmed with crape. The heat did not seem to you to be any excuse.

The only amusement which she had enjoyed with her husband had been riding. Until the last day of his life Baron Philipot, a champion horseman, rarely missed his morning ride. Marinette had her mare brought to Calèse, and, as nobody could escort her, she went riding alone, which struck you as doubly scandalous. A widow of three months ought not to take any exercise in any case; but that she should go riding without a bodyguard passed all bounds.

"I shall tell her what we think of it in the family," you kept on saying. You told her, but she went on having her own way. Finally, tired of fighting, she asked me to escort her. She undertook to get a very quiet mount for me. (All the expenses, of course, were to fall on her.)

We used to start at dawn, because of the flies, and because we had to go for two kilometres at a walk before reaching the nearest pine-woods. The horses awaited us at the steps. Marinette put out her tongue at the closed shutters of your room as she pinned on to her habit a rose drenched with dew—"Not at all the thing for a widow," she said. The bell of the first Mass rang in short strokes. Abbé Ardouin greeted us shyly, and disappeared in the mist that floated over the vineyards.

Until we reached the woods, we used to talk. I realised that I had some prestige in the eyes of my sister-in-law— less on account of my standing as a barrister than for the subversive ideas of which I made myself the champion in the family. Your principles resembled those of her husband too much. To a woman, religion, ideas, are always somebody; everything takes a shape in her eyes: a shape adorable or hateful.

I had only to press my advantage with this little rebel. But lo and behold!—so long as she confined her irritation to you, I had no difficulty in reaching her pitch; but it was impossible for me to follow her in the contempt she showed in the matter of the millions which she would lose if she married again. It was entirely to my interest to talk as she did and play the noble-hearted part; but it was impossible for me to make a pretence of it. I could not even look as though I approved when she reckoned the loss of that inheritance as nothing.

Must I confess it?—I did not even succeed in driving away

the thought of her death, which would make us her heirs. (I was not thinking about the children, but about myself.)

I might do my best to prepare myself in advance and repeat my lesson: the thing was too much for my strength of will.

"Seven millions! Marinette, you can't think of it; one doesn't give up seven millions. There isn't a man in the world worth the sacrifice of even a part of that fortune!" And, when she claimed that she put happiness above everything, I assured her that nobody could be happy after the sacrifice of a sum like that.

"Oh," she cried, "what's the sense of your hating them? You belong to the same species."

She set off at a gallop, and I followed her at a distance. I was judged; I had lost. That mad taste for money—what has it not spoiled for me! I might have found in Marinette a little sister, a friend. . . .

And you expect me to sacrifice the one thing to which I have sacrificed everything else? No, no, my money has cost me too dearly for me to abandon a halfpenny of it to you before I breathe my last sigh.

Yet you are tireless. I wonder whether Hubert's wife, to whose visit I had to submit on Sunday, was delegated by you, or came of her own accord. That poor Olympia! (Why did Phili nickname her Olympia? In any case we have forgotten her real name. . . .)

I rather think that she said nothing to you about her approach to me. You have not adopted her; she is not a woman of the family. This person, indifferent to everything which does not constitute her narrow world, which does not touch her directly, is not familiar with the laws of the "tribe"; she does not realise that I am the enemy. It is not kindness or natural sympathy on her part: she never thinks of other people, even to hate them.

"He is always very nice to me," Olympia protests when my name is mentioned before her. She does not feel my hardness; and, as it happens that, out of a spirit of contradiction, I defend her against all of you, she has persuaded herself that she attracts me.

From her confused conversation, I gathered that Hubert had unloaded in time, but that all his personal property and his wife's dowry had been required to meet his commitments. "He says that he is bound to get his money back, but that he needs an advance. . . . He calls it an advance on inheritance."

I nodded my head, I assented, I pretended to be a thousand miles away from understanding what she wanted. How innocent I am, at times like that!

If poor Olympia only knew what I had sacrificed for money, when I still had a little of my youth left! On those mornings of my thirty-fifth year, we used to come back, your sister and I, letting our horses walk, along the road between the sulphated vines. To that mocking young woman I talked about the millions that she must not lose. When I escaped from the haunting thought of those menaced millions, she laughed at me with contemptuous friendliness. When I tried to defend myself, I plunged in deeper.

"It is in your own interest that I insist, Marinette. Do you think I am the kind of man to be obsessed by his children's future? Isa, if you like, does not want your fortune to disappear from under their noses. But I . . ."

She laughed, clenched her teeth a little, and ventured: "It's true that you're horrid enough."

I protested that I was thinking only of her happiness. She shook her head with disgust. Fundamentally, without her confessing it to herself, it was maternity, rather than marriage, that she wanted.

She despised me. But after lunch, when, despite the heat, I left the dark, cool house where the family drowsed, stretched out on leather couches and wicker chairs; when I half opened the heavy shutters of the French window and slipped out into the blue on fire, I did not need to turn round: I knew that she would come too. I heard her steps in the gravel. She walked badly, twisting on her high heels on the hard surface. We leant over the parapet of the terrace. She invented a game of keeping her bare arm on the burning stone as long as possible.

The plain, at our feet, surrendered itself to the sun in a silence as deep as when it sleeps in the moonlight. On the horizon the Landes formed an immense black arc, on which the metallic sky weighed down. Not a man, not a beast would emerge until the fourth hour. The flies quivered where they lay, no less immobile than the single smoke in the plain, which no breath of wind stirred.

I knew that this woman who stood there beside me could not love me, that there was nothing about me which was not hateful to her. But we alone were breathing, in that enchanted estate, within a barrier of torpor. This young, suffering human being, closely watched by a whole family, sought my eyes as unconsciously as a heliotrope turns towards the sun.

Nevertheless, to the smallest disturbing word I should have received no other reply but a mockery. I knew very well that she would repulse the shyest approach with disgust. So we stood there side by side, on the edge of that immense vat in which the future grape-harvest fermented in the sleep of leaves turning blue.

And you, Isa—what did you think about those morning rides, those colloquies at an hour when the rest of the world reposed? I know what you thought, because one day I overheard you. Yes, through the closed shutters of the drawing-room I heard you telling your mother, who was staying at Calèse (and had come there, no doubt, to reinforce the watch on Marinette):

"He has a bad influence over her, from the point of view of ideas . . . but otherwise, he occupies her, and there's no harm in it."

"Yes, he occupies her; that's the essential thing," replied your mother.

You were both pleased that I should occupy Marinette. "But after the holidays," you said more than once, "we must think of something else."

Whatever contempt I may have inspired in you, Isa, I despised you much more for saying that. No doubt you did not imagine that there could be the least danger. Women never remember what they no longer experience.

After lunch, on the edge of the plain, it was true, nothing could happen; for, empty though the world was, we were both, so to speak, as though we stood before a drop-screen. Even if it were only a peasant who did not surrender himself to siesta, he would have seen, as motionless as lime-trees, that man and that woman facing the incandescent earth, who could not have made the least movement without touching one another.

But our nocturnal walks were less innocent. I remember an evening in August. Dinner had been stormy on account of Dreyfus. Marinette, who, together with myself, represented the re-trial party, had now surpassed me in the art of routing out Abbé Ardouin and compelling him to take sides. After you had spoken with exaltation about an article of Drumont's, Marinette, in her voice of a child at catechism, inquired:

"Monsieur l'Abbé, is it permissible to hate the Jews?"

That evening, to our greater joy, he did not resort to vague evasions. He spoke about the greatness of the Chosen People, their exalted rôle as a witness, their predicted conversion, the forerunner of the end of time. And when Hubert protested that one must hate the executioners of Our Lord, the abbé replied that every one of us had a right to hate but one executioner of Christ: "Ourselves, and nobody else."

Taken aback, you retorted that, with these fine theories, there was nothing to be done but hand over France to the foreigners. Happily for the abbé, you went on to Jeanne d'Arc, who reconciled you. From the steps one of the children cried: "Oh, what a lovely moon!"

I went out on to the terrace. I knew that Marinette would follow me. As a matter of fact, I heard her low-voiced "Wait for me. . . ." She came out with a "boa" round her neck.

The full moon was rising in the east. Marinette admired the long oblique shadows of the elms on the grass. The peasants' houses bore the brightness with closed eyes. Dogs were barking. She asked me whether it was the moon that made the trees so still. She said to me that everything was created, on such a night, for the torture of the lonely.

"An empty setting!" she said. How many lips were united at that hour, how many shoulders close together, how much intimacy!

I saw, quite clearly, a tear trembling on her lashes. In the immobility of the world, there was nothing living but her breath. It always came a little panting. . . .

What remains of you this evening, Marinette, dead in 1900? What remains of a body buried these thirty years? I remember the scent of you that night. To believe in the resurrection of the flesh, perhaps one must have conquered the flesh. The punishment of those who abuse it is that they cannot even imagine that it will rise again.

I took her hand, as I might have taken that of an unhappy child; and, like a child, she leant her head on my shoulder. I took her because I was there, as the soil takes a peach that falls. Most human beings choose one another scarcely more than trees which grow side by side, whose branches merge through their mere growth.

But what was infamous in me, at that moment, was that I thought of you, Isa; that I dreamt of a possible revenge: to make use of Marinette to make you suffer. Fleetingly as the idea flashed through my mind, it is nevertheless true that I conceived this crime.

We took a few uncertain steps out of the zone of moonlight, towards the thicket of pomegranate-trees and syringa. Fate would have it that, just then, I heard a sound of footsteps in the vinewalk—that path which Abbé Ardouin followed every morning on his way to Mass. It was he, no doubt. . . .

I thought of what he had said to me one evening: "You are very good. . . ." If he could have read my heart at that moment! Was it, perhaps, the shame that I felt which saved me?

I took Marinette back into the moonlight, and made her sit down on a bench. I dried her eyes with my handkerchief. I said to her what I might have said to Marie, if she had fallen and I had picked her up, in the lime-tree walk. I pretended not to have noticed whatever there might have been a little disturbing in her abandon and in her tears.

Chapter IX

THE next morning she did not go out riding. I went to Bordeaux (I used to go and spend two days a week there, despite the legal vacation, so as not to discontinue my consultations).

When I was catching the train to return to Calèse, the Southern Express was in the station, and great was my astonishment to see, through a window of the coach labelled "Biarritz," Marinette, without a veil, wearing a grey tailor-made costume. I remembered that a friend of hers had been pressing her for some time to go and stay with her at Saint Jean de Luz. She was looking at an illustrated paper, and did not notice my signals.

That evening, when I told you about this, you paid little attention to what you took to be only a brief break. You said that, shortly after I left, Marinette had received a telegram from her friend. You seemed surprised that I did not know all about it. Did you, perhaps, suspect us of a clandestine meeting in Bordeaux?

In any case, little Marie was in bed with fever. She had been suffering, for some days, from a looseness of the bowels that made you anxious. I owe it to you to say that, when one of your children was ill, nothing else mattered.

I should like to pass quickly over what followed. After more than thirty years, it is only with an immense effort that I can bear to think about it.

I know of what you accuse me. There is no doubt about it that, if we had called in Professor Arnozan, he would have diagnosed a typhoid condition in that supposed attack of influenza. But think over your recollections. Just once, you suggested to me: "Suppose we call in Arnozan?" I answered you: "Doctor Aubrou says that he is dealing with more than a score of cases of the same type of influenza in the village. . . ." You did not even press the point.

You claim that you begged me, the very next day, to telegraph to Arnozan. I should remember it if you had done so. It is true that I chewed the cud of those memories to such an extent, for days and nights, that I cannot find my way about in them now. Let us agree that I was a miser . . . but not to the point of being mean when it was a question of Marie's health. It is by so much the less likely since Professor Arnozan worked for love of God and mankind. If I did not call him in, it was because we were sure that it was merely an attack of influenza "which had gone to her bowels."

That fellow Aubrou made Marie eat to keep up her strength. It was he who killed her; it was not I. No, we were quite agreed. You never insisted that we should get Arnozan, you liar. I am not responsible for Marie's death. It's horrible that you should accuse me of it; and you believe it! You have gone on believing it.

That pitiless summer! The delirium of that summer, the insistence of the grasshoppers! . . .

We could not succeed in getting any ice. For endless afternoons I wiped her little sweating face that drew the flies. Arnozan came too late. We changed the treatment only when she was utterly lost.

Perhaps she was delirious when she repeated: "For Papa! For Papa!" You remember how she cried: "My God, I am only a child . . ." and then she went on: "No, I can still bear it." Abbé Ardouin gave her Lourdes water to drink.

Our heads came together over that exhausted body, our hands touched. When it was all over, you thought that I had no feeling.

Do you want to know what was going on inside me? It is a strange thing that you, the Christian woman, could not tear yourself away from the corpse. They begged you to eat something; they kept on telling you that you would need all your strength. But they had to use force to get you out of the room. You stayed sitting there right up against the bed. You touched her brow, her cold cheeks, with groping hands. You put your lips to that still living hair; and sometimes you fell on your knees, not to pray, but to lean your forehead upon those stiff, icy little hands.

Abbé Ardouin lifted you up, and talked to you about those children who one must be like to enter into the Kingdom of the Father. "She is alive; she can see you, she is waiting for you." You shook your head; these words did not even reach your brain; your faith served you for nothing.

You thought only of that flesh of your flesh which was going to be buried, and was on the eve of corruption; while I, the unbeliever, in the presence of what remained of Marie, felt all that is signified by the word "remains."

I had the irresistible sense of a departure, of an absence. She was not there any more; it was not she any more. "Seek ye Mary? She is no longer here. . . ."

Later, you accused me of forgetting quickly. But I know what snapped in me when I kissed her, for the last time, in her coffin.

It was not she any more, though. You despised me because I would not go with you to the cemetery, where you went nearly every day. "He never sets foot in it," you kept on saying. "And yet Marie was the only one he seemed to love a little. He has no heart."

Marinette came back for the funeral, but she left again three days later. Pain blinded you. You did not see the danger that threatened you in that direction. But still, you had the air of being relieved by your sister's departure.

Two months later, we had the news of her engagement to that man of letters, the journalist whom she had met at Biarritz. It was too late to ward off the blow. You were implacable—as though a hatred that you had suppressed suddenly burst forth against Marinette. You refused to know that "person"—quite an ordinary man, like any number of others. His only crime was that he baulked your children of a fortune, from which he derived little advantage himself, since most of it went to Philipot's nephews.

But you never reasoned. You never had the shadow of a doubt. I never knew anybody who could be so serenely unfair as you. God knows what peccadilloes you confessed!— and there was not a single one of the Beatitudes which you did not spend your life in denying. You had no scruples about assembling false witness to fling at the objects of your hatred—as in the case of your sister's husband, whom you had never seen, and about whom you knew nothing at all. "She was the victim, at Biarritz, of a fortune-hunter, one of those hotel rats, you know. . . ." That was what you said.

When the poor girl died in childbirth (no, no, I don't want to judge you as harshly as you judged me about Marie!) it is not enough to say that you showed scarcely any regret. Events had put you in the right: it was bound to end like that; she had gone to her death; you had nothing with which to reproach yourself; you had done everything you possibly could; the unfortunate girl knew perfectly well that her family would always take her back into its bosom, that it was ready for her, that she had only to lift a finger.

At least you could do yourself that much justice: you had nothing whatever to do with it. It had cost you something to be firm; "but there are times when one has to trample on one's feelings."

No, I don't want to reproach you. I recognise that you were good to Marinette's son, to little Luc, once your mother, who looked after him until her death, was no longer there to concern herself about him. You took charge of him during the holidays. You went to see him, once every winter, at his school outside Bayonne. You "did your duty, since his father would not do his. . . ."

I have never told you how I came to meet Luc's father, at Bordeaux, in September, 1914. I was looking for a safe-deposit at a bank. Parisians in flight had taken all there were. Finally the manager of the Crédit Lyonnais told me that one of his clients was going back to Paris, and might let me have his. When he told me the client's name I discovered that it was Luc's father with whom I had to deal.

Oh no, he was not the monster whom you imagined! I sought in vain, in that man of thirty-eight, emaciated, haggard, gnawed by the fear of being conscripted after all, him whom I had met at Marinette's funeral and with whom I had talked about business. He talked to me quite openheartedly. He was living, in marital relations, with a woman with whom he wanted to spare Luc contact. It was in the boy's interest that he had turned him over to his grandmother Fondaudège. . . .

My poor Isa, if you had only known, you and the children, what I offered that man, that day! I don't mind telling you now. He was to keep the safe in his own name; I was to have his power of attorney. All my disposable fortune was to be deposited there, with a document attesting that it belonged to Luc. As long as I lived, his father was not to touch the safe. But after my death, he was to take possession of it, and you would have known nothing about it. . . .

Obviously I should have been handing myself over to the man, myself and my fortune. How I must have hated you at that moment! Well, he didn't choose to do it. He didn't dare. He talked about his honour.

How could I have been guilty of such a madness? At that time, the children were approaching thirty, they were married, they were definitely on your side, turned against me on every possible occasion. You were working in secret: I was the enemy.

God knows that with them, with Geneviève especially, you were not on the best of terms. You reproached her with leaving you always alone, with never consulting you about anything. But against me the common front was established.

Everything passed off, for that matter, in a minor key, except on solemn occasions. Then there were terrible battles, such as over the children's marriages. I did not want to give them a dowry, but merely an income. I did not choose to let the families concerned know the state of my fortune. I gained my point, I had the whip hand, and hatred made me firm—hatred, but also love: the love that I had for Luc. The families concerned put up with it, in any case, because they had no doubt that the fortune was enormous.

But my silence made you anxious. You wanted to be sure. Geneviève tried sometimes to get on the soft side of me—that poor clumsy fool, whom I could hear clattering along in her clogs from miles away! Often I said to her: "When I am dead, you will bless me," just for the pleasure of seeing her eyes gleam with greed. She repeated those miraculous words to you. The whole family went into a trance.

Meanwhile I was seeking a means of leaving you nothing except what it was impossible to hide. I thought only of little Luc. I even had the idea of mortgaging the land. . . .

Well, after all, it happened once that I let myself be taken in by your pretences. It was during the year that followed Marie's death. I fell ill. Certain symptoms recalled those of the disease that had carried away our little one. I detest being nursed, and I have a horror of doctors and medicines. You never rested until I reconciled myself to going to bed and getting Arnozan.

You nursed me devotedly, that goes without saying, but also anxiously, and sometimes, when you asked me how

I was feeling, it seemed to me that what I could discern in your voice was pain. When you put your hand on my brow, you did it in the same way as for the children. You wanted to sleep in my room. If I was restless during the night, you got up and gave me a drink.

"She's fond of me," I thought; "who would have believed it? . . . Is it because of what I make, perhaps?" But no, you didn't love money for itself. . . . Unless it was that the children's position would be disimproved by my death? That seemed more likely. But it wasn't that, either.

After Arnozan had examined me, you talked to him on the terrace, with that rise in your voice which has given you away so often.

"Please tell everybody, Doctor, that Marie died of typhoid. Because of the death of my two poor brothers, it got about that it was consumption which carried her away. People are so nasty, they will never let go of a thing. I tremble to think that this may do the gravest harm to Hubert and Geneviève. If my husband had been seriously ill, it would have given substance to all this gossip. He made me anxious for some days: I was thinking about the children.

"He, too, you know, had an affected lung before his marriage. That's known; everybody knows it; people take such pleasure in these things! Even if he died of an infectious disease, they wouldn't believe it, any more than they did in Marie's case. And my poor little ones would have to pay for it.

"It made me mad when I saw him taking such little care of himself. He wouldn't even go to bed! As though he had nobody to think about but himself! But he never thinks of anybody else, not even the children. . . . No, no, Doctor, a man like you couldn't believe that men like him exist. You're just the same as Abbé Ardouin, you never think evil of anybody."

I laughed all to myself, in my bed, and, when you came

back, you asked me why. I answered you in these words, in current use between us: "Oh, nothing."

"What are you laughing about?"—"Oh, nothing."

"What are you thinking about?"—"Oh, nothing."

Chapter X

I return to this document after an attack which has held me at the mercy of all of you for nearly a month. As soon as illness disarms me, the family circle presses closer round my bed. There you all are, watching me.

Last Sunday, Phili came to keep me company. It was hot; I answered in monosyllables; I lost the thread of ideas. . . . For how long? I cannot say. The sound of his voice aroused me. I saw him in the dimness, with his ears pricked up. His young wolf's eyes were gleaming. On his forearm, above his wrist-watch, he wore a gold chain. His shirt was half-open over his childlike chest.

I fell into a stupor again. The creaking of his shoes awakened me, and I watched him through half-closed lids. His hand was groping at my jacket, in the neighbourhood of the inside pocket where I keep my note-case. My heart pounded madly, but I forced myself to remain motionless. Were his suspicions aroused? He went back to his chair.

I pretended to awaken. I asked him whether I had been asleep long.

"Just a few minutes, Grandfather."

I experienced that terror of lonely old men when a young man lurks around them. Am I going mad? It seemed to me that the fellow was capable of killing me. Hubert admitted, one day, that Phili was capable of anything.

Isa, you see how wretched I am. It will be too late, when you read this, for you to show me any pity. But it comforts me to hope that you may feel a little. I do not believe in your everlasting Hell; but I know what it is to be damned upon this earth, to be a man reprobated, a man who, whichever way he goes, goes the wrong way; a man who has always gone the wrong way: somebody who does not know how to live—not at least in the sense in which worldly people understand living; somebody who lacks the art of life in the absolute sense of the phrase.

Isa, I'm suffering. The south wind burns up the air. I am thirsty, and I have nothing but the lukewarm water in the dressing-room. I have millions, but not a glass of cold water.

If I endure the presence of Phili, terrifying though it is to me, the reason, perhaps, is that he reminds me of another boy, a boy who would be in his thirties by now, little Luc, our nephew. I have never denied your virtues; and that boy gave you occasion to exercise them. But you did not love him: there was nothing of the Fondaudèges about him, about that son of Marinette, that boy with his jet-black eyes, with his hair growing low on the forehead and smoothed down on the temples in "kiss-curls," as Hubert called them.

He was not a good worker, at that school in Bayonne where he was a boarder. But that, you used to say, was no business of yours. It was quite enough that you had to take charge of him during the holidays.

No, it wasn't books that interested him. In this country-side, where there is next to no game, he still succeeded in bringing down something almost every day. The hare, the only hare of the year, that had its lair on our land—he always ended by laying it at our feet. I can still see his triumphant gesture in the main path through the vineyard, his clenched fist holding the beast with its bleeding snout by the ears. I used to hear him setting off at dawn. I opened my window; and his fresh voice came to me through the mist: "I'm going to pick up my night-lines."

He used to look me straight in the face, his eyes did not fall before mine, he was not afraid of me. Such an idea never entered his head.

If, after I had been away for a day or two, I came back

unexpectedly and smelt an odour of cigars about the house; if I found the drawing-room without a carpet and all the signs of an interrupted party—as soon as my back was turned, Geneviève and Hubert invited friends, organised "surprise-parties," despite my formal prohibition; and you were an accomplice in their disobedience, "because," you said, "one must return hospitality . . ."—in these cases, it was always Luc who was sent to me, to disarm me.

He found the terror which I inspired comic. "I went into the drawing-room while they were dancing and shouted: 'Here's uncle! He's coming by the short-cut . . .' You should have seen them pack up! Aunt Isa and Geneviève rushed the sandwiches into the pantry. What a scamper!"

He was the only person in the world, that boy, to whom I was not a bugbear. Sometimes I went down to the river with him when he was fishing. Always running and jumping at other times, he could stay motionless, for hours, waiting, transformed into a willow—and the movements of his arm were as slow and silent as those of a branch.

Geneviève was right when she said that he wasn't "literary." He never troubled himself to go and see the moonlight on the terrace. He had no "feeling" for Nature because he was Nature itself, merged in it, one of its forces, one of its living springs among other springs.

I used to think of all the elements of tragedy in his young life: his mother dead, that father of his who must not be mentioned among us, his boarding-out, his loneliness. Very much less would have made me overflow with bitterness and hatred. But joy gushed out of him. Everybody was fond of him. How strange that seemed to me—me, whom everybody hated! Everybody loved him, even I. He smiled at everybody, and also at me; but not more than at anybody else.

In that utterly instinctive being, what struck me most of all, as he grew up, was his purity, his ignorance of evil, his disregard of it. Our children were good children, I must admit. Hubert was a model boy, as you put it. In that respect, I recognise that your education bore fruit. But if Luc had had time to become a man, would he have given as little trouble?

Purity, in him, did not seem to be acquired or conscious. It shone upon him, like the dew upon the grass. If I linger over this, it is because it awakened an echo deep down within me. Your paraded principles, your assumptions, your airs of disgust, your pursed mouth would never have given me any consciousness of evil, such as was conveyed to me by that boy, all unknown to myself. It was not until long afterwards that I realised this.

If humanity, as you imagine, bears upon it the brand of original sin, no human eye could have discerned it in Luc. He emerged from the hands of the potter intact and perfect in his grace. But I—in his presence I could feel my own deformity.

Should I say that I cherished him like a son? No, for what I loved in him was that I did not see myself in him. I know very well what Hubert and Geneviève have got from me: that greed of theirs, that primacy in their life of temporal possessions, that capacity for contempt (Geneviève treats Alfred, her husband, with an implacability which bears my mark). In Luc, I was sure of not bumping up against myself.

During the rest of the year I scarcely thought of him. His father looked after him during the Christmas and Easter holidays, and the long vacation brought him back to us again. He left our countryside in October, with the other birds.

Was he pious? You said of him: "Even in a little animal like Luc, one finds the influence of the Fathers. He never misses his Communion on Sundays. . . . I admit that his act of contrition does not take him long; but, after all, nobody is asked for more than he has it in him to give."

He never talked to me about such things; he never made the least allusion to them. His conversation was always about the most concrete matters. Sometimes, when he pulled out of his pocket a knife, a float or a whistle to lure larks, his little black rosary fell on the grass, and he picked it up again quickly. Perhaps, on Sunday mornings, he seemed a little quieter than on other days, less volatile, less imponderable, as though charged with an unknown substance.

Among all the links that bound me to Luc, there was one that will surprise you a little. It happened sometimes, on those Sundays, that I recognised, in that young faun who leapt no longer, the brother of the little girl who fell asleep a dozen years earlier, our Marie, very different from him as she was—she who could not bear one to kill an insect, whose greatest pleasure it was to carpet the hollow of a tree with moss and place a statue of the Virgin there—don't you remember?

All the same, in Marinette's son, in him whom you called the little animal, it was our Marie who came to life for me again—or, rather, the same spring that burst forth in her, and that went underground again with her, welled up at my feet once more.

When the war broke out, Luc was not quite fifteen. Hubert was mobilised in the auxiliary services.

The medical boards, before which he appeared philosophically, gave you anxious moments. Upon the narrowness of his chest, which had given you nightmares for years, all your hopes now depended. When the monotony of office life, and also some jeers, inspired him with a keen desire to see active service, and he made some moves in that direction, you went so far as to talk openly about what you had been at such pains to dissimulate. "With his throwback . . ." you kept on saying.

My poor Isa, don't be afraid of my throwing stones at you. I never interested you, and you never paid any attention to me; but, during that period, you did so even less than at any other time. You had no idea how anxiety rose in me as the campaign went on through the winter. Luc's father had been mobilised for civil service, and we had the boy with us not only during the long vacation, but also for Christmas and Easter. The war filled him with enthusiasm. He was afraid that it would be over before he reached the age of eighteen.

He, who had never opened a book before, devoured military text-books, studied maps. He developed his body methodically. At the age of sixteen, he was already a man —a hard-trained man. There was a fellow who had no tears to shed over the wounded or the dead! Out of the saddest stories about life in the trenches that I gave him to read, he made up for himself the image of a terrible, magnificent sport, which one would not always have the right to play. He would have to hurry.

Oh, how afraid he was of being too late! He already had the authorisation of his idiot of a father in his pocket. And I, as his fatal birthday on January 18 approached—I followed old Clemenceau's career feverishly, I watched it like those parents of prisoners who looked forward to the fall of Robespierre, hoping that the tyrant would fall before their sons came up for judgment.

When Luc was in camp at Souges, during his period of instruction and training, you sent him woollens and dainties; but you used some words that awakened the instinct of murder in me, my poor Isa, when you said: "Poor young fellow, of course it would be very sad . . . but he, after all, wouldn't leave anybody behind him. . . ." I know that you did not mean to hurt when you said this.

One day, I realised that there was no hope that the war would come to an end before Luc went to it. When the front was broken on the Chemin des Dames, he came to say good-bye to us, a fortnight earlier than he expected.

Well, I must pluck up courage here to recall a horrible memory, which still awakens me at night and makes me cry aloud. That day I went to my study to get a leather belt, specially made by the harness-maker from a model which I had given him myself. I climbed on a stool and tried to pull towards me the plaster head of Demosthenes which stood on top of my book-case. I could not move it. It was full of gold pieces which I had hidden there after mobilisation. I plunged my hand into that gold, the thing to which I was most attached in the world, and I stuffed the leather belt full of it. When I got down off the stool, that boa-constrictor, swollen with metal, was hanging round my neck and bearing down upon my nape.

I offered it shyly to Luc. He did not understand at first what I was giving him.

"What do you expect me to do with that, Uncle?"

"It will be useful to you in billets, or if you are taken prisoner . . . or in lots of other circumstances. One can always do something with money."

"Oh," he said, with a laugh, "I have enough to carry with all my kit. . . . How do you suppose I could load myself down with all that gold? The first time I go up the line I should have to hide it in the woods."

"But, my dear fellow, at the beginning of the war everybody who had any gold took it with him."

"That was because they didn't know what they were in for, Uncle!"

He was standing up in the middle of the room. He had thrown the belt of gold on the couch. That strong boy— how frail he looked in a uniform too big for him! From its gaping collar emerged his drummer-boy's neck. His cropped hair robbed his face of any character of its own. He was prepared for death, he was "all correct" like so many others, indistinguishable, already anonymous, already vanished.

For an instant his eyes fixed themselves on the belt; then he handed it back to me with an expression of mockery and contempt. He kissed me, though.

We went to see him off at the door. He turned round to shout to me to "take all that to the Bank of France." I could not see anything any more. I heard you laughing and saying to him:

"Don't be too sure of that! It's too much to ask him!"

The door closed, and I stood motionless in the hall. You said to me:

"Confess that you knew he wouldn't take your gold. It was an empty gesture."

I remembered that I had left the belt on the couch. A servant might find it; one never knows. I hurried upstairs, and put it around my shoulders again to empty its contents into the head of Demosthenes.

I scarcely noticed the death of my mother, which occurred a few days later. She had been half-witted for years, and was no longer living with us.

It is now that I think of her, every day, the mother of my childhood and my youth: the image of what she became is effaced. I, who detest cemeteries, go to her grave sometimes. I do not take any flowers now, for I found that they were stolen. The poor go and sneak roses for the benefit of their own dead. I should have to go to the expense of a railing; and everything is so dear nowadays.

Luc, for his part, has no grave. He disappeared; he was a "missing." I have in my note-case the only letter he had time to send me: "Everything all right, have received parcel. Love." He wrote: "love." At least I got that word from my poor child.

Chapter XI

TO-NIGHT a choking feeling awakened me. I had to get up and drag myself to my chair. There, in the tumult of a howling wind, I read over these last few pages—stupefied by the backgrounds in myself which they illuminated.

Before writing any more, I leant at the window. The wind had dropped. Calèse slept without a breath under all the stars. Suddenly, about three hours after midnight, again there came a squall, rumblings in the sky, heavy, icy raindrops. They rattled on the slates to such an extent that I was afraid they were hail. I thought my heart had stopped beating.

The vines have barely "passed their flower." The future harvest covers the slopes. But it seems that its fate may be that of those young animals which the hunter ties up and leaves in the darkness to attract beasts of prey. Growling clouds are prowling around the exposed vines.

But what does the harvest matter to me now? I have nothing left to harvest in this world. I can only learn to know myself a little better.

Listen, Isa. Among my papers you will discover, after my death, my last wishes. They date from the months that followed the death of Marie, when I was ill and you were concerned about the children. You will find in them a profession of faith couched in terms something like these:

"If, at the time of my death, I accept the ministry of a priest, I protest in advance, being in full possession of my faculties, against the abuse which will have been made of my mental and physical weakness to obtain of me that which my reason rejects."

Well, I owe you this confession: it is, on the contrary,

when I study myself, as I have been doing for the past two months, with a curiosity which is stronger than my disgust; it is when I feel myself most fully in possession of my faculties that the Christian temptation torments me. I can no longer deny that a route exists in me which might lead me to your God.

If I succeeded in being satisfied with myself, I could combat this demand upon me better. If I could despise myself unreservedly, the issue would be decided once and for all. But the hardness of the man I am, the dreadful destitution of his heart, this gift which he possesses of inspiring hatred and creating a desert around himself—none of these things prevails against hope. . . .

Can you believe me, Isa? Perhaps it was not for you, the righteous, that your God came, if He did come, but for us. You have never known me; you have never known the kind of man I was. These pages that you have read—have they made me less hateful in your eyes? You must see, at least, that there exists in me a secret chord: that which Marie set vibrating, simply by nestling in my arms; and also little Luc, on Sundays, when he came back from Mass, sat down on the bench in front of the house, and gazed at the meadow.

Oh, above all don't imagine that I have any very high idea of myself! I know this heart of mine—this heart; this tangle of vipers. Stifled under them, steeped in their venom, it goes on beating under the swarming of them: this tangle of vipers that it is impossible to separate, that needs to be cut loose with a slash of a knife, with the stroke of a sword. "I am not come to bring peace, but a sword."

To-morrow, it may be that I shall deny what I confess to you here, as I have denied, this night, my last wishes of thirty years ago. I have seemed to hate with an undying hatred all that you profess, and I still continue to hate those who arrogate to themselves the name of Christians; but is it not because so many of them demean a hope, disfigure a countenance, that Countenance, that Face?

By what right do I judge them, you will ask me—I, who am an abomination? Isa, is there not in my baseness something that resembles, more than their virtue does, the Sign that you adore?

What I have just written is doubtless, in your eyes, a preposterous blasphemy. You must prove it to me. Why do you not speak to me? Why have you never spoken to me? Is there, perhaps, some word of yours that would open my heart?

To-night, it seems to me that it is not yet too late to begin our lives over again. What if I do not wait until I am dead to hand over these pages to you? What if I adjured you, in the name of God, to read them to the end? What if I saw you coming back to my room, with your face bathed in tears? What if you opened your arms to me? What if I asked your pardon? What if we fell on our knees together?

The storm seems to be over. The stars that herald the dawn are fluttering. I thought that it was raining again, but it was the drops falling from the leaves. If I lie down on my bed, would I stifle again? In any case, I cannot write any more, and sometimes I lay down my pen and let my head loll against the hard back. . . .

A hiss like that of a beast, then a great din, together with a glare, have filled the sky. In the panic silence that followed, bombs have burst on the slopes, exploded by the vine-growers to scatter the hail-clouds or dissolve them into water. Fusees have gone up from that corner of the darkness where Barsac and Sauternes tremble in expectation of the scourge. The bell of Saint Vincent's, which drives away the hail, is tolling at top speed, like somebody who sings at night because he is afraid—and, suddenly, on the slates, that noise like a handful of pebbles. . . .

Hail! Once I would have leapt to the window. I hear

shutters being flung open. You have just shouted to a man hurrying across the courtyard: "Is it bad?" He replied: "Luckily it's mixed with rain, but it's coming down hard." A frightened child has run barefoot down the passage.

I have calculated by force of habit: "A hundred thousand francs lost. . . ." But I have not stirred. Once nothing would have kept me back from going out—just as when they found me, one night, in the midst of the vines, in my slippers, with a blown-out candle in my hand, letting the hail fall on my head. Some profound peasant instinct drove me there, as though I sought to stretch myself out and cover the stoned vines with my body.

But to-night—here I am, become a stranger to what used to be, in the deepest sense, my virtue. At last I am detached. I do not know what, I do not know who, has detached me, Isa, but the cables are broken: I am drifting.

What force is drawing me? A blind force? Love? Perhaps love. . . .

PART THE SECOND

Chapter XII

Paris, Rue Bréa.

WHAT made me put this document in my baggage? What have I to do now with this long confession? All is over between me and my family. She for whose benefit I have been exposing myself here in all my nakedness can no longer exist for me. What is the good of going on with this work?

It is that sub-consciously, perhaps, I find a consolation, a sense of deliverance, in it. What a light those last lines, written on the night of the hail, shed upon me! Must I not have been on the brink of madness?

No, no, let me not speak of madness here! Let madness not even be named. They are capable of making use of it against me, if these pages should fall into their hands.

These pages are no longer addressed to anybody. I must destroy them as soon as I feel that I am getting worse . . . unless I bequeath them to that unknown son whom I came to seek in Paris. I was burning to reveal his existence to Isa, in those pages where I referred to my love affair of 1909. I was on the point of confessing that my mistress went away pregnant, to hide herself in Paris. . . .

I thought that I was being generous because I sent the mother and child six thousand francs a year, before the war. The idea of increasing this sum never entered my head. It is my own fault if I have found here two enslaved human beings, diminished by degrading toil.

Because they live in this district, I am staying at a boarding-house in the Rue Bréa. Between the bed and the wardrobe, I have hardly room to sit down to write. Besides, what a din! In my time Montparnasse was quiet. Now it seems to be inhabited by mad people who never go to bed.

The family was making less noise on the steps at Calèse, that night when I saw with my own eyes, heard with my own ears. . . .

What is the good of going back on that? Still, it would be a relief to pin down that cruel memory, even if only for a little time. . . . For that matter, why should I destroy these pages? My son, my heir, has a right to know me. Through this confession I should be lessening, to some small extent, the distance at which I have kept him ever since he was born.

Alas! two meetings with him sufficed for me to make up my mind about him. He is not a man to find the least interest in this document. What could he make of it, that clerk, that understrapper, that dull fellow who bets on horses?

During the night journey from Bordeaux to Paris, I imagined the reproaches which he would address to me and prepared my defence. How one lets oneself be influenced by the cheap conventions of the novel and the theatre! I was sure that I should have to deal with an illegitimate son full of bitterness and grandeur of soul. Sometimes I endowed him with the hard nobility of Luc, sometimes with Phili's good looks. I was prepared for anything, except that he should resemble me. Are there any fathers to whom it is a pleasure to be told: "Your son is so like you?"

I measured the hatred which I have for myself when I saw this spectre of myself rise before me. I cherished, in Luc, a son who did not resemble me. There is only one respect in which Robert differs from me: he has shown himself incapable of passing any examination whatever. He had to give up any hope of doing so, after repeated failures. His mother, who had worked herself to death, despises him for it. She cannot refrain from rubbing it in. He hangs his head. He cannot get over the loss of all that money. In that respect he is certainly my son.

But what I have to offer him, this fortune of mine, is beyond the limits of his narrow imagination. It does not mean anything to him; he simply cannot believe in it. As a matter of fact, his mother and himself are afraid. "It's not legal. . . . We might be caught. . . ."

That fat, washed-out woman, with faded hair, that caricature of her whom I loved, looks at me with eyes still very beautiful. "If I had met you in the street," she tells me, "I wouldn't have known you. . . ."

And I—should I have known her? I was afraid that she might be resentful, revengeful. I was prepared for anything, except this dreary indifference of hers. Soured, dulled by eight hours a day of typewriting, she is afraid of scandal. She has retained a sickly dread of the Law with which she once got into trouble.

Yet I have explained the procedure to them clearly. Robert takes a safe in his own name at a bank. I deposit my fortune there. He gives me his power of attorney to open the safe, and undertakes not to touch it himself until my death. Naturally I require him to sign a declaration that everything the safe contains belongs to me. After all, I cannot put myself in the hands of this stranger. The mother and son object that, when I am dead, this document will be found. The fools are not prepared to trust me.

I have tried to make them understand that we can rely upon a country lawyer like Bourru, who owes everything to me, and with whom I have done business for forty years. He has in his care an envelope on which I have written: "to be burned the day of my death," and which will be burned, I am quite sure, with all it contains. In it I will put Robert's declaration. I am the better assured that Bourru will burn it, inasmuch as that sealed envelope contains documents which he has an interest in seeing out of the way.

But Robert and his mother are afraid that, after my death, Bourru will not burn anything and proceed to blackmail them. I have thought of that, too: I will put in their own hands evidence that will send Bourru to prison if he blinks an eye. The document will be burned by Bourru in their presence, and only then will they surrender to him the weapon with which I shall provide them. What more do they want?

They simply cannot grasp it. There they are, pig-headed, that idiot and that imbecile, to whom I offer millions and who, instead of grovelling at my feet, as I expected, go on arguing, cavilling. . . . What if there is a bit of a risk? The game is well worth the candle. But no—they will not sign the paper. "It would be bad enough with the income-tax people, to start with. . . . We should get into difficulties. . . ."

Oh, how I must hate the others, that I don't slam the door in their faces, the two of them! They are afraid of the "others," too. "They'll find out. . . . They'll bring an action against us. . . ." Already Robert and his mother imagine that my family has put the police on the alert, and that I am being watched. They refuse to see me except at night or in out-of-the-way places. As though, in my state of health, I could sit up all night and spend my life in taxis!

I do not believe that the others are suspicious. This is not the first time that I have been away alone. They have no reason to believe that the other night, at Calèse, I was present, unseen, at their council of war. In any case, they have not tracked me down yet. This time there is nothing to prevent me from attaining my end. If only Robert would agree to act, I could sleep in peace. But the coward will not take the risk.

This evening, July 13, an orchestra is playing in the open air. At the end of the Rue Bréa couples are dancing. Oh, for peaceful Calèse! I remember the last night I spent there. Despite the doctor's prohibition, I had taken a tablet of veronal, and I slept soundly.

I awakened with a start and looked at my watch. It was an hour after midnight. I was startled to hear several voices. My window was open. There was nobody in the courtyard, or in the drawing-room. I went into the dressing-room, which faces north, on the same side as the steps. It was there that the family, contrary to their custom, were sitting up late. At that late hour they had no suspicion of anybody overhearing them. Only the windows of the dressing-room and the passage open in that direction.

The night was still and warm. In the intervals of silence, I could hear Isa's rather short breathing, the scraping of a match. Not a breath of wind stirred the black elms. I did not dare to lean out, but I could recognise each of my enemies by his or her voice and laugh. They were not arguing. A remark from Isa or Geneviève was followed by a long silence. Then suddenly, at a word from Hubert, Phili flared up, and they were all talking at once.

"Are you quite sure, Mamma, that the safe in his study contains only papers of no value? A miser is always imprudent. Remember that gold he wanted to give young Luc. . . . Where was he hiding it?"

"No, he knows that I know the combination of the safe, which is: 'Marie.' He never opens it except when he has to consult an insurance policy or a tax return."

"But, Mother, it might give us a clue to the sums he is hiding."

"There is nothing there but papers relating to the estate, I am quite sure of it."

"And that's terribly significant, don't you think? It makes one feel that he has taken all possible precautions."

Phili murmured, with a yawn:

"Oh, what a crocodile! Just my luck to have stumbled upon a crocodile like that!"

"And if you want to know what I think," declared Geneviève, "you won't find anything in the safe at the Crédit Lyonnais, either. What do you say, Janine?"

"But after all, Mamma, one would say, sometimes, that he loves you a little. When you were young, didn't he ever show himself kind? No? None of you has ever known how to take him. You haven't been very clever. One should have got round him, made a conquest of him. I could have done that, I am sure, if he hadn't such a horror of Phili."

Hubert interrupted his niece sourly:

"It is certainly true that your husband's rudeness is going to cost us dearly."

I heard Phili laugh. I leant out a little. The flame of a match lit up his two hands, his smooth chin, his thick lips for a moment.

"Come, come, he didn't wait for me to have a horror of you!"

"No, but before then he didn't dislike us so much. . . ."

"Remember what Grandmamma told us," Phili went on, "his attitude when he lost his little girl. . . . He didn't seem to care. . . . He never set foot in the cemetery. . . ."

"No, Phili, you're going too far. If he ever loved anybody in the world, it was Marie."

But for that protest of Isa's, made in a faint, trembling voice, I should not have been able to restrain myself. I sat down on a low chair, leaning forward, with my head against the window-sill. Geneviève was speaking.

"If Marie had lived, none of all this would have happened. At the worst he would only have favoured her. . . ."

"Come, come, he would have got his claws into her like everybody else! He's a monster. He has no human feelings."

Isa protested again:

"I must ask you, Phili, not to speak about my husband like that before me and his children. You owe him some respect."

"Respect? Respect?"

He muttered something like:

"If you think it's fun for me to have got into a family like this. . . ."

"Nobody asked you to," his mother-in-law told him drily.

"But such expectations were flashed before my eyes. . . . Hullo, here's Janine crying! What's the matter? What have I said wrong now?"

He growled: "Oh, come now!" on a note of exasperation. I heard nothing more than Janine sniffling. A voice which

I could not identify murmured: "What stars!" The clock of Saint Vincent's struck two.

"Children, we must go to bed."

Hubert protested that they could not break up the meeting without having settled anything. It was high time to act. Phili backed him up. He did not think that I could last much longer. Then there would be nothing to be done. I would have laid all my plans. . . .

"But after all, my poor children, what do you expect me to do? I've tried everything. I can't do any more."

"Yes, you can!" said Hubert. "You could very well. . . ."

What was he whispering? I was missing the very thing I most wanted to know. From Isa's tone I gathered that she was shocked, scandalised.

"No, no, I wouldn't like to do that!"

"It's not a question of what you would like, Mamma, it's a question of saving our patrimony."

There were more indistinct murmurs, cut short by Isa.

"It's very hard, my child."

"But Grandmamma, you can't go on being his accomplice. He can disinherit us only with your permission. Your silence implies approval of him."

"Janine, my dear, how dare you? . . ."

Poor Isa, who had spent so many nights at the bedside of that little cry-baby; who had taken her into her own room, because her parents wanted to get some sleep and no nurse would put up with her! . . . Janine was talking sharply, in a tone which would have sufficed to make me beside myself. She added:

"It hurts me to say these things to you, Grandmamma. But it is my duty."

Her duty! That was what she called the demands of her flesh, her terror of being deserted by that blackguard whose idiotic laugh I could hear. . . .

Geneviève backed up her daughter. It was quite true that weakness might amount to being an accomplice. Isa sighed.

"Perhaps, my children, the best thing would be to write to him."

"Oh, no, not a letter, above all!" protested Hubert. "Letters always let us down. I hope you haven't written to him already, Mamma?"

She confessed that she had written to me, two or three times.

"Not letters of threats or insults?"

Isa hesitated about admitting it. And I—I laughed to myself. . . . Yes, indeed, she had written to me: letters that I had carefully preserved, two which contained the gravest insults, and a third almost affectionate, quite enough to make her lose any suit for separation which her fools of children might try and persuade her to bring against me. They were all disturbed now, as when one dog growls and the rest of the pack start growling.

"You haven't written anything like that, Grandmother? He hasn't got any letter which might be dangerous to us?"

"No, I don't think so. . . . Well, there was once when Bourru—that little lawyer at Saint Vincent, whom my husband must have under his thumb in some way or other (but he's a cad and a hypocrite)—said to me: 'Oh, Madame, you were very imprudent to write to him. . . .'"

"What did you write to him? No insults, I hope?"

"Just once—some rather violent reproaches, after Marie's death. And then there was another time, in 1909: it was about a liaison more serious than the others."

When Hubert groaned: "That's bad, that's very bad!" she thought to reassure him by telling him that she had settled matters all right afterwards, that she had expressed her regrets, recognised that she was in the wrong.

"Oh, for Heaven's sake, that puts the lid on it! . . ."

So there was no fear of a separation suit now. . . .

"But what makes you think, after all, that his intentions are so black for us?"

"Why, they stare you in the face!—the impenetrable mystery of his financial operations; the hints he dropped; what he let slip to Bourru, before a witness: 'They'll make a face, when the old man dies . . .'"

They went on talking as though the old woman were no longer there. She got up from her chair with a groan. It was wrong of her, with her rheumatism, she said, to sit outside at night. The children did not even answer her. I heard some careless "Good-nights" that they threw her without interrupting their conversation. It was she who had to go the rounds and kiss them; they did not disturb themselves.

I went back to bed, to be on the safe side. Her heavy steps echoed on the staircase. She came to my door, and I could hear her breathing. She put her candle down on the floor, and opened the door. She was quite close to my bed. She bent over me, doubtless to make sure that I was asleep. What a long time she stayed! I was afraid of giving myself away. Her breath was coming short. Finally she shut my door again. When she had locked her own, I went back to the dressing-room, to my listening-post.

The children were still there. They were talking in low voices now. Many of their words escaped me.

"He wasn't of her social position," Janine was saying. "There was that, too. Phili, my dear, you're coughing. Put your coat on."

"Really, it isn't his wife he hates most; it's us. You couldn't imagine such a thing, could you? It's something you don't find even in books. It is not for us to judge our mother," Geneviève wound up, "but I think that Mamma isn't hard enough on him. . . ."

"Well, of course" (it was Phili's voice), "she'll always get her dowry back. Her father Fondaudège's Suez shares . . . those must have gone up since 1884. . . ."

"The Suez shares? But they're sold. . . ."

I recognised the hesitancy, the hemming and hawing, of Geneviève's husband. It was the first remark that poor

Alfred had made. Geneviève interrupted him, in that bitter, nagging tone which she keeps for him.

"Are you mad? The Suez shares sold?"

Alfred related how, in the month of May, he had gone to see his mother-in-law and found her in the act of signing papers. She had said to him: "It seems that this is the moment to sell them. They are at the peak, they'll go down."

"And you never told us?" cried Geneviève. "What a fool you are! He made her sell her Suez shares? And you tell us that as though it were the most ordinary thing in the world! . . ."

"But Geneviève, I thought that your mother kept you in touch with things. In any case, by the marriage settlement she remained mistress of her own property. . . ."

"Yes, but won't he pocket the profits of the transaction? What do you think about it, Hubert? Imagine his never telling us! And that's the man I've had to spend my life with. . . ."

Janine intervened to ask them to speak lower: they would waken her little girl. For a few moments I could hear nothing more. Then Hubert's voice became distinguishable again.

"I've been thinking about what you were saying just now. We can't try anything in that direction, through Mamma. At least, we should have to lead her up to it, little by little. . . ."

"She might rather have that than separation. Since separation would necessarily end in divorce, a case of conscience arises. . . . Of course, what Phili proposes seems shocking at first sight. But, after all, we are not the judges. It is not we who decide in the last resort. Our rôle is limited to getting the thing started. It would only happen if it is recognised as necessary by the competent authorities."

"And I tell you that it would be a wasted effort," declared Olympia.

Hubert's wife must have been out of all patience to raise

her voice as she did. She asserted that I was a man with all his wits about him, of very sound judgment, "with whom," she added, "I may say that I often agree, and I could twist him round my finger, if you didn't undo all my work. . . ."

I did not hear what rude reply Phili made; but they all laughed, as they always do whenever Olympia opens her mouth. I caught snatches of sentences.

"For the last five years he hasn't pleaded—he hasn't been able to plead."

"Because of his heart?"

"Yes, now. But when he left the Law Courts he was not yet very ill. The truth is that he had rows with his colleagues. There were scenes in the lobbies, about which I already have some evidence. . . ."

I stretched my ears in vain. Phili and Hubert had drawn their chairs together. I could hear only an indistinct murmur, then this exclamation from Olympia:

"Oh, I say! The only man here to whom I can talk about what I read, with whom I can exchange general ideas—you want to. . . ."

Out of Phili's reply I caught the word "daft." One of Hubert's sons-in-law—the one who hardly ever speaks—said in a tone of stifled rage:

"Please show some manners to my mother-in-law."

Phili protested that he was only joking. Weren't they both victims in this business? When Hubert's son-in-law declared, still in a voice that trembled, that he did not regard himself as a victim and that he had married his wife for love, there was a general chorus: "So did I! So did I! So did I!" Geneviève said to her husband mockingly:

"Oh, you too!—are you bragging that you married me without knowing what my father's fortune was worth? Just you remember the evening of our engagement! Didn't you whisper to me: 'What does it matter if he won't tell us anything about it, when we know it's enormous?'"

There was a general burst of laughter, an uproar. Hubert raised his voice again, and was the only one to speak for a few moments. I could hear only the last sentences.

"It's a question of justice, a question of morality, which over-rides everything else. We are defending the patrimony, the sacred rights of the family."

In the deep silence that precedes the dawn, their conversation came to me more distinctly.

"Have him watched? He is too well in with the police, I have proof of that. He would be warned. . . ." Then, a few moments later: ". . . His hardness, his greediness, are common knowledge. One may go so far as to say that his honesty has been called in question in one or two cases. But so far as sound understanding, mental balance, are concerned. . . ."

"In any case, nobody can deny the inhuman, the monstrous, the unnatural character of his feelings towards us. . . ."

"If you think, my little Janine," said Alfred to his daughter, "that that will suffice to obtain a certification. . . ."

I was beginning to understand. I had already understood. A great calm reigned in me, a sense of peace born of this certitude: it was they who were the monsters, and I who was the victim.

Isa's absence gave me pleasure. She had more or less protested, as long as she had been there; and, before her, they had not dared to make any reference to the project which I had just overheard—and which did not frighten me in the least.

Poor fools! As though I were the kind of man to let myself be put under restraint or shut up! Before they could raise a hand against me, I could very soon place Hubert in a desperate position. He did not realise my hold upon him. As for Phili, I have a file. . . . The idea of making use of it had never occurred to me. But I shall not need to make use of it. It will be enough for me to show my teeth.

For the first time in my life, I experienced the satisfaction of being the least bad. I had no desire to avenge myself upon them. Or, rather, I wanted no other vengeance beyond that of snatching away from them that heritage over which they pined away with impatience and sweated with anxiety.

"A shooting star!" cried Phili. "I had no time to make a wish."

"One never has time," said Janine.

Her husband went on, with that gaiety of a child which he had retained:

"When you see one, cry: 'Millions!'"

"What an ass you are, Phili!"

They all got up. The garden chairs rasped on the gravel. I heard the locking of the front door, Janine's stifled laughter in the passage. The doors of the bedrooms shut one after the other.

My decision was taken. For the last two months I had had no attack. There was nothing to prevent me from going to Paris. As a rule, I went away without saying anything about it. But I did not want this departure to resemble a flight. Until morning I went over the plans I had already made. I put them in order.

Chapter XIII

WHEN I got up at midday, I did not feel in the least tired. Bourru, summoned by telephone, came after lunch. We walked up and down, for nearly three-quarters of an hour, under the lime-trees. Isa, Geneviève and Janine watched us from a distance, and I enjoyed their anxiety. What a pity that the men were in Bordeaux!

They said of the little old lawyer: "Bourru is his usual self." Wretched Bourru, whom I hold more tightly than any slave! It was a sight to see the poor devil, that morning, struggling against my giving a weapon against him to my eventual heir. "But," I told him, "inasmuch as he will give it up, as soon as you have destroyed the receipt signed by him. . . ."

When he left, he made a deep bow to the ladies, who barely responded, and got on his bicycle with his tail between his legs. I joined the three women, and told them that I was leaving for Paris that evening. Isa protested that it was rash for me to travel alone in my state of health.

"I really must see about my investments," I replied. "Though I may not look like it, I am thinking about you."

They looked at me with an anxious air. My ironical tone gave me away. Janine glanced at her mother, and plucked up her courage.

"Grandmother or Uncle Hubert could go instead of you, Grandfather."

"That's a good idea, my child—quite a good idea; but there it is: I have always been in the habit of doing things for myself. Besides, it's a bad thing, I know, but I don't trust anybody."

"Not even your children? Oh, Grandfather!"

She emphasised the word "grandfather" in a rather affected way. She assumed a coaxing, irresistible air. Oh, that exasperating voice of hers, that voice which I had heard during the night, mingling with the others! . . .

Then I burst out laughing—that dangerous laugh which makes me cough, and visibly terrified them. I shall never forget poor Isa's face, her worn-out appearance. She must have had to withstand some pressure already. Janine would probably return to the charge, as soon as my back was turned. "Don't let him go, Grandmamma. . . ."

But my wife was in no condition to attack. Her race was run, and her weariness was too much for her. I had heard her saying to Geneviève, the other day: "I should like to lie down, and sleep, and never waken up. . . ."

She saddened me, now, as my poor mother had saddened me. The children were trying to bring into action against me this old, used-up machine, incapable of serving them. Still, they loved her, in their own way. They forced her to see the doctor, to be careful about her diet.

Her daughter and her grand-daughter moved away, and she came closer to me.

"Listen," she said, very quickly, "I want some money."

"This is the 10th. I gave you your month's allowance on the 1st."

"Yes, but I had to lend money to Janine. They are very hard up. I save money out of the housekeeping; I'll give it back to you out of the August allowance."

I replied that it was no affair of mine, and that I was not going to support that fellow Phili.

"I have overdue accounts at the butcher's, the grocer's. . . . Look, here they are."

She pulled them out of her handbag. I felt sorry for her. I offered to sign cheques for them; "in that way I should be sure that the money did not go elsewhere. . . ." She agreed to that. As I took out my cheque-book, I noticed Janine and her mother watching us from the rose-walk.

"I'm sure," I said, "that they think you are talking to me about something else. . . ."

Isa trembled. She asked in a low voice: "What else?" At that moment I felt that tightening of my chest. I put my two hands together to it in the way that she knew so well. She came close to me.

"Are you in pain?"

I held on to her arm for a moment. We looked, there in the middle of the lime-tree walk, like an old married couple who were ending their lives together after years of deep unitedness. I murmured in a low voice: "I'm better now." She must have thought that this was the time to speak, a unique opportunity. But she had no strength left. I noticed that she, too, was fighting for breath. Actually ill as I was, I had made an effort. She had let herself go, surrendered; there was nothing of her left.

She sought for something to say, and looked furtively towards her daughter and grand-daughter to give herself courage. In the eyes that she turned back to me I read an indescribable weariness, perhaps pity, and certainly a little shame. The children must have hurt her, that night.

"I'm anxious about your going away alone."

I told her that if anything happened to me on the way, she might spare herself the trouble of having me brought back. And, when she begged me not to say things like that, I added:

"It would be an unnecessary expense, Isa. Cemetery soil is the same everywhere."

"I feel the same as you do," she sighed. "Let *them* put me where they like. Once I wanted so much to sleep beside Marie . . . but what is there left of Marie?"

Once more I realised that, to her, her little Marie meant that dust, those bones. I did not dare to protest that I, for years, had felt my child to be alive; that I breathed the atmosphere of her; that she often crossed the darkness of my life, like a sudden gust of wind.

In vain did Geneviève and Janine keep watch upon her;

Isa seemed tired of trying. Did she measure the nothingness of what she had fought for, all these years? Geneviève and Hubert, urged on themselves by their own children, had set against me this old woman, Isa Fondaudège, the scented girl of the nights of Bagnères.

For nearly half a century we had been confronting one another. Yet now, in that heavy afternoon, we two adversaries felt the link which, despite that long struggle, was created by our participation in old age. Seeming to hate one another, we had reached the same point. There was nothing, there was nothing any more beyond that promontory where we awaited death. There was nothing for me, at least. For her there still remained her God; her God must still remain for her.

All that she had held as doggedly as myself fell away from her all at once: all those desires which had interposed themselves between her and the Infinite Being. Could she see Him now, Him from Whom nothing separated her any more?

No; there remained to her the ambitions, the demands of her children. She was charged with the fulfilment of their desires. She had to start being hard all over again as a proxy. Anxiety about money, health, calculations based on ambition, on jealousy—all this was there before her, like a student's homework on which the master writes: "To be done again."

She turned her eyes again towards the walk where Geneviève and Janine, armed with pruning scissors, were pretending to trim the roses. From the bench where I had sat down to get my breath again, I watched my wife going away from me, with her head down, like a child on its way to be scolded. The excessive heat of the sun heralded a storm. She walked with the steps of those to whom walking means suffering. I imagined I could hear her moaning: "Oh, my poor legs!" An old married couple never hate one another as much as they think.

She had rejoined her children, who were evidently addressing reproaches to her. Suddenly I saw her coming towards me again, red in the face, breathless. She sat down beside me and groaned.

"This stormy weather tires me. I've very high blood-pressure, these days. . . . Listen, Louis, there is something I'm anxious about. Those Suez shares of my dowry—how have you reinvested them? I remember that you asked me to sign some papers. . . ."

I told her the figure of the enormous profit which I had realised for her, just before the shares went down. I explained to her how I had reinvested the sum in bonds.

"Your dowry has littered, Isa. Even if one takes account of the depreciation of the franc, you ought to be dazzled. Everything is in your own name, at the Westminster Bank, your original dowry and the profits. . . . The children will not be disappointed—you may set your mind at rest about that. I am the master of my own money and of what my own money has produced; but what comes from yours belongs to you. Go and reassure those angels of unselfishness down there."

She caught my arm suddenly.

"Why do you dislike them so much, Louis? Why do you hate your family?"

"It is all of you who hate me. Or, rather, my children hate me. You—you ignore me, except when I irritate you or frighten you. . . ."

"You might add: 'Or when I torture you.' Don't you think I have suffered in my time?"

"Come, come! You had no eyes except for the children. . . ."

"I had to attach myself to them. What was left for me apart from them?" She went on in a lower voice. "You neglected me and betrayed me from the very first year, you know very well."

"My poor Isa, surely you are not asking me to believe

that my little truancies hurt you very much—except, perhaps, in your pride as a young wife?"

She laughed bitterly.

"How sincere you sound! When I think that you never even took any notice of me. . . ."

I trembled with hope. It is a strange thing to say, since it was a question of feelings that were done with, ended. The hope of having been loved, forty years earlier, unknown to myself . . . but no, I could not believe it. . . .

"You never had a word, never a greeting, for me. The children sufficed for you."

She buried her face in her two hands. I had never noticed their big veins, their speckles, so much as that day.

"My children! When I think that, from the moment when we started having separate rooms, I deprived myself for years of having any of them with me at night, even when they were ill, because I was always waiting, hoping that you would come."

Tears ran down her old hands. It was Isa. I alone could still find, in that stout, almost invalid old woman, the girl devoted to white, on the road in the Lys valley.

"It's shameful, it's ridiculous at my age to recall such things. . . . Yes, above all, it's ridiculous. Forgive me, Louis."

I gazed at the vineyard without answering. A doubt came to me, at that moment.

Is it possible for us, for nearly half a century, to observe only one side of the person who shares our life? Can it be that, out of habit, we pick and choose among the things they say and the things they do, retaining only that which nurtures our grievances and perpetuates our resentment? Have we a fatal tendency to simplify other people—to eliminate all those features which might be regarded as extenuating, which might render more human the caricature of them which our hatred needs for its justification? . . .

Did Isa see how upset I was? She was too quick to try and score a point.

"You're not going away this evening?"

I thought I could see that light in her eyes, when she believed that she had "got me." I feigned surprise, and said that I had no reason for putting off my journey. We went back to the house together. On account of my heart, we did not take the slope through the elms, but followed the lime-tree walk that runs round the house.

In spite of everything, I remained uncertain and upset. Suppose I did not go? Suppose I gave Isa this document? Suppose. . . .

She laid her hand on my shoulder. How many years was it since she had done that? The walk emerges in front of the house, on the North side. Isa said:

"Cazau never puts the garden chairs straight. . . ."

I gave a casual glance. The empty chairs still formed a close circle. Those who had occupied them had felt the need of drawing together to talk in low voices. The ground was cut up by their heels. Everywhere there were butts of the cigarettes that Phili smokes.

The enemy had camped there, the night before. They had held council under the stars. They had talked there, in front of my own house, opposite the trees planted by my father, about putting me under restraint or shutting me up.

One night of humility, I had compared my heart with a tangle of vipers. No, no; the tangle of vipers was outside myself. They had gone out of me and rolled themselves together, that night. They formed that hideous circle at the foot of the steps, and the earth still bore their traces.

You will get your money back, Isa, I thought to myself, your money that I have made fruitful; but nothing more than that—not another thing. And even the estate—I would find a way to prevent them from having that. I would sell Calèse; I would sell all my land. Everything that came from my family should go to that unknown boy with whom, to-morrow, I would have an interview.

Whatever he might be, he did not know all of you. He had taken no part in your plots. He had been brought up away from me, and he might not hate me; or, if he did hate me, the object of his hatred would be an abstract be-ing, without relationship with myself. . . .

I shook myself free angrily and hurried up the steps, for-getful of my old, weak heart. Isa cried: "Louis!" I did not even look back.

Chapter XIV

I could not sleep, and I dressed again and went out into the street. To reach the Boulevard Montparnasse, I had to make a way for myself through the midst of dancing couples. Formerly even a Republican as good as myself shunned the fêtes of July 14. The idea of taking part in the pleasures of the street did not enter the head of any respectable man.

This evening, in the Rue Bréa and in front of the Rotonde, it is not corner-boys who are dancing. There is nothing debauched about them; they are healthy young fellows, bareheaded, some of them wearing open-necked shirts with short sleeves. Among the girls dancing there are few prostitutes.

The crowd hangs on to the mud-guards of taxis that interrupt its sport, but good-humouredly and without offence. A young man, whom I jostled by accident, cried: "Make room for the old gentleman!" I passed between a double row of shining faces. "Aren't you sleepy, Grandfather?" a dark boy, with his hair growing low on his forehead, laughed into my face.

Luc would have learned to laugh like that, and to dance in the street; and I, who have never known what it is to let myself go, to amuse myself, would have learned how to do so from my poor boy. He would have been more overflowing with joy than anybody else; he would not have lacked for money. . . . It was with earth that his mouth was filled. . . .

So ran my thoughts while, with my chest racked by the familiar pain, I sat on the terrace of a café right in the middle of the fun.

And suddenly, amid the crowd that flowed between the pavements, I saw myself. It was Robert, with a shabby-looking comrade. Those long legs of Robert's, that chest narrow as my own, that head sunk in his shoulders—how I hate them! In him all my defects are accentuated. I have a long face, but his is as long as that of a horse—the face of a hunch-back. His voice, too, is that of a hunch-back.

I called him. He left his comrade, and looked around him with an anxious air.

"Not here," he said to me. "Come and meet me on the right-hand pavement, in the Rue Campagne-Première."

I pointed out to him that we could not be better hidden than in the midst of this hubbub. He let himself be persuaded, took leave of his comrade, and sat down at my table.

He had a sporting paper in his hand. To start a conversation I made an effort to talk about horses. Long ago I had to do so with old Fondaudège. I told Robert that, when my father-in-law bet, he took considerations of the most widely differing kinds into account: not merely the far-back pedigree of the horse, but also the nature of the ground that suited it best. . . . He interrupted me.

"As for me, I get tips at Dermas's"—this was the draper's shop where he had relapsed into a job, in the Rue des Petits-Champs.

He added that the only thing that interested him was winning. Horses bored him. "Give me bicycles," he said; and his eyes shone.

"Very soon," I told him, "it will be motorcars. . . ."

"Imagine that!"

He wetted his thumb, pulled out paper and tobacco, and rolled a cigarette. There was a silence. I asked him whether the business depression was making itself felt in the shop where he worked. He told me that part of the staff had been dismissed, but that he was in no danger himself. Never did his thoughts go outside the narrowest circle of his personal interests. It was into the lap of this dullard that millions were to fall.

"Suppose I gave them to charity," I thought, "suppose I gave them away myself? No, *they* would have me put under restraint. . . . By my will? It was impossible to exceed the stipulated proportion. Ah, Luc, if only you were alive! . . . It is true that he would not have accepted, but I should have found a means of enriching him without his suspecting that it was I—for example, by giving a dowry to the girl with whom he would have fallen in love. . . ."

"Listen, Monsieur. . . ."

Robert stroked his cheek with a red hand, with pudgy fingers.

"I've been thinking things over. Suppose that lawyer, Bourru, died before the paper was burned. . . ."

"Well, his son would succeed him. The weapon which I shall give you against Bourru would serve equally well, if the case arose, against his son."

Robert went on stroking his cheek. I made no attempt to say anything more. The tightness in my chest, that torturing contraction, was enough to occupy me.

"Listen, Monsieur. . . . Take this case. . . . Bourru burns the paper; I hand over to him the one which you have given me to compel him to keep his word. But after that, what is to prevent him from going to your family and saying to your children: 'I know where the fortune is. I will sell you my secret. I ask so much for revealing it, and so much more if you are successful?' He could make it a condition that his name should not appear. . . .

"From that moment he would run no further risk. There would be an inquiry. It would be discovered that I am really your son, and that my mother and myself had changed our way of life since your death. . . . And of two things one: either we shall have made correct declarations for income-tax purposes, or else we shall have falsified them. . . ."

He spoke quite clearly. His mind lost its sluggishness. Slowly his reasoning-machine had started working, and there was no stopping it. What remained powerful in this counter-jumper was the peasant instinct of looking ahead, of distrust, of horror of taking risks, of anxiety to leave nothing to chance. No doubt he would have preferred to take a hundred thousand francs passed from hand to hand, rather than have to conceal that enormous fortune.

I waited until my heart felt freer and the sense of constriction passed off.

"There is something in what you say. Very well, I'll agree to this: you will not sign any document. I will trust you. For that matter, it would always be easy for me to prove that this money belongs to me. Not that it is of much importance—in six months, in a year at the most, I shall be dead."

He made no gesture of protest; he could not find the commonplace expression that anybody else would have used. It was not that he was harder than any other young fellow of his age. Simply, he was badly brought up.

"In that case," he said, "it might be done."

He ruminated over the idea for a few moments, and added:

"I should have to go to the safe from time to time, even while you were alive . . . so that they would get to know my face, at the bank. I could go and get money for you. . . ."

"As a matter of fact," I interjected, "I have more than one safe abroad. If you prefer it, if you think it would be less risky. . . ."

"What, leave Paris?"

I pointed out to him that he could go on living in Paris and make trips when it was necessary. He asked me whether the fortune was in securities or in liquid form, and went on:

"All the same I should like you to write me a letter to the effect that, being of sound mind, you freely bequeath your fortune to me. . . . In case the truth came out and I

133

were accused of theft by the others—one never knows. Besides, to keep my conscience quiet. . . ."

He stopped again, bought some pea-nuts which he started gobbling, as though he were hungry, and added suddenly:

"As a matter of fact, what have they done to you, the others?"

"Take what I offer you," I replied coldly, "and ask no questions."

A little blood flushed his colourless cheeks. He smiled that nettled smile of his, with which he was doubtless accustomed to meeting the reprimands of his employer, and so disclosed his sound, well-shaped teeth, the only redeeming feature in that graceless face.

He went on shelling pea-nuts, without saying anything more. He did not seem to be dazzled. Clearly his imagination was working. I had stumbled upon the one person in the world capable of seeing nothing but the very small risks in this prodigious boon. I wanted to dazzle him at all costs.

"Haven't you a mistress?" I asked him point-blank. "You could marry her, you could live like rich middle-class people."

He made a vague gesture and shook his head sadly. I was persistent.

"For that matter, you could marry anybody you liked. If there is a girl of your acquaintance who seems out of your reach. . . ."

He pricked up his ears, and for the first time I saw the flame of youth shine in his eyes.

"I could marry Mademoiselle Brugère!"

"Who is Mademoiselle Brugère?"

"No, I was joking. A shopwalker at Dermas's—think of that! A fine girl! She doesn't even look at me; she doesn't even know that I exist. . . . Just think of that!"

I assured him that, with a twentieth part of his fortune, he could marry any "shopwalker" in Paris.

"Mademoiselle Brugère!" he repeated. Then he shrugged his shoulders. "No, it's not to be thought of. . . ."

I had a pain in my chest again. I beckoned to the waiter. Then Robert did an astonishing thing.

"No, Monsieur, please—I can at least offer you this."

I put the money back into my pocket with satisfaction. We got up. The musicians were packing up their instruments. The garlands of electric lights had been extinguished. Robert need no longer be afraid of being seen with me.

"I'll walk home with you," he said.

I asked him to walk slowly, on account of my heart. I was lost in admiration of the fact that he did nothing to hasten the execution of our plans. I told him that, if I died that night, he would lose a fortune. He gave a shrug of indifference. All I had done was to confuse the fellow.

He was about my own height. Would he ever have the air of a gentleman? He seemed so paltry, this son and heir of mine!

I tried to give our conversation a more intimate turn. I assured him that I could never think without remorse of the poverty in which I had left them, him and his mother. He seemed surprised. He found it "very handsome" that I should have given them a regular income. "There are many who would not have done as much." He added a horrible remark: "After all, you were not the first. . . ." Clearly he did not judge his mother indulgently. When we reached my door, he said to me suddenly:

"Here's an idea. . . . Suppose I got a job which would compel me to frequent the Stock Exchange. . . . That would explain my fortune."

"Don't do anything of the kind," I told him. "You would lose everything."

He stared down at the pavement with a preoccupied air. "It's about the income-tax; if the inspector made inquiries. . . ."

"But when this is liquid money, an anonymous fortune,

deposited in safes which nobody on earth has a right to open, except yourself. . . ."

"Yes, of course, but all the same. . . ."

I slammed the door in his face in exasperation.

Chapter XV

Calèse.

THROUGH the window against which a fly is buzzing, I look out at the stricken slopes of the vineyards. The wind moans as it brings up heavy clouds, whose shadow glides across the plain. This silence of death signifies the universal expectation of the first rumbling. "The vines are afraid," Marie said, one sad summer's day thirty years ago, a day like this.

I have re-opened this note-book. It is certainly my hand-writing. I examine its characters closely, the trace of the nail of my little finger beneath the lines.

I shall go on with this narrative to the end. I know now for whom I intend it. I must finish this confession; but I shall have to suppress a good many pages, whose reading would be too much for them.

As for myself, I cannot read them over again straight through. Every other moment, I interrupt myself and bury my face in my hands. Here is a man, here is a man among men, here am I. You may spew me forth. I exist just the same.

That night, the night of July 13 to July 14, when I had parted from Robert, I scarcely had the strength to undress and lie down on my bed. An enormous pressure stifled me; and, despite this stifling, I could not die. The window was open: if I had been on the fifth floor . . . but, from the first, I could not kill myself. That was the only considera-tion which restrained me. I could barely stretch out my hand to take the pills which as a rule, relieve me.

At dawn, they finally answered my bell. A local doctor gave me an injection, and I got my breath again. He or-dered absolute immobility. Excessive pain makes us more submissive than little children. I had no difficulty about keeping still. The ugliness, the mouldy smell of that room, of that furniture, the noise of that stormy July 14—none of these things mattered to me, so long as I was no longer in pain. I asked nothing more than that.

Robert came to see me one evening, and did not reappear. But his mother came and spent a couple of hours with me, when she left her office, did me a few small services, and brought me my letters from the *poste restante*. There was no letter from my family.

I made no complaints, I was very docile, I drank everything I was told. She turned the conversation when I talked to her about our plans. "There is no hurry," she kept on saying. I sighed: "There is the proof that there is a hurry," and pointed to my heart.

"My mother lived to the age of eighty, and she had attacks much worse than yours."

One morning, I found myself better than I had been for some time. I was very hungry, and the stuff they gave one to eat in that boarding-house was uneatable. I decided to go and lunch at a little restaurant in the Boulevard Saint-Germain, where I liked the cooking. The bill there caused me less astonishment and anger than at most of the other eating-places, where I generally sat down in terror of spending too much.

A taxi deposited me at the corner of the Rue de Rennes. I took a few steps to test my strength. All went well. It was barely noon. I decided to go and drink a glass of Vichy at the "Deux Magots." I sat down inside, on the bench up against the window, and looked out casually at the boulevard.

I felt my heart miss a beat. On the terrace, separated from me by the thickness of the glass, those narrow shoulders, that bald patch, that hair going grey at the nape, those round ears, sticking out from the head. . . . There was Hubert, with his short-sighted eyes reading a paper and his nose nearly touching its pages.

Obviously he had not seen me coming in. The beating of my weak heart calmed down. A frightful joy possessed me: I was spying upon him, and he did not know that I was there.

The last place where I should have expected to see Hubert was on a café terrace on the Boulevards. What was he doing in this part of Paris? He had certainly not come there without some definite object. I had nothing to do but wait, I paid for my Vichy at once, so that I could get up and leave as soon as might be necessary.

Clearly he was expecting somebody. He kept on looking at his watch. I thought I had guessed who was going to manœuvre among the tables to reach him, and I was almost disappointed when I saw Geneviève's husband getting out of a taxi.

Alfred had his straw hat on the side of his head. Away from his wife, that fat little man in his forties reverted to type. He was wearing too light a suit, and was shod in too bright shoes. His provincial idea of elegance contrasted with the quiet clothes of Hubert, who, as Isa said, "dressed like a Fondaudège."

Alfred took off his hat and mopped his shining forehead. He swallowed the apéritif that was brought him at a gulp. His brother-in-law was already on his feet, looking at his watch. I prepared to follow them. No doubt they would take a taxi. I would take another and try to follow them: a difficult matter. Still, it was a good deal in itself to have discovered that they were in Paris.

I waited to go out until they were at the edge of the pavement. They made no sign to any chauffeur, and crossed the square. Still talking, they went towards the church of Saint-Germain-des-Prés. What a surprise, what a joy! They went into the church. A policeman, who sees a thief walking into a trap, does not experience a more delightful feeling than the one that nearly choked me, at that moment.

I took my time. They might turn round; and, if my son was short-sighted, my son-in-law was sharp-eyed. Despite my impatience, I forced myself to wait two minutes on the pavement; then, in my turn, I entered the porch.

It was a little after midday. I advanced with precaution into the almost empty nave. It did not take me long to assure myself that those for whom I was looking were not there. For a moment that idea flashed through my mind that perhaps they had seen me, and that they had only come in to throw me off the scent and had gone out by one of the side doors. I went back on my tracks and made my way along one of the lateral aisles, that on the right, hiding behind the enormous pillars.

Suddenly, in the darkest part of the apse, with their backs to the light, I saw them. Sitting on chairs, they hemmed in a third person, with humble, drooping shoulders, whose presence did not surprise me. It was the very man whom I had just expected to see gliding towards the table of my legitimate son. It was my other son, that poor larva, Robert.

I had foreseen the possibility of this betrayal; but I had not let my mind rest upon it, through sheer weariness, sheer laziness. From our very first meeting it had struck me that this sorry creature, this born slave, lacked guts, and that his mother, haunted by memories of trouble with the police, might advise him to come to terms with the family and sell his secret at the best possible price.

I looked at the back of that idiot's head. He was firmly embedded between those two gentlemen of substance, one of whom, Alfred, was what is called good-hearted—though at the same time very keen on his own interests, taking a short view, but it paid him—and the other, my dear little Hubert, was a grasping fellow, with a decisive air of authority about him, which he got from me, and against which Robert would be powerless.

I observed them from behind a pillar, as one watches a spider trapping a fly, when one has already made up his mind to destroy both spider and fly. Robert was hanging his head lower and lower. He had probably begun by saying to them: "Share and share alike. . . ." He thought he had the whip hand. But, by the mere act of making himself known to them, the fool had put himself in their power, and there was nothing for him to do but take what he could get.

And I, witness of this struggle which I alone knew to be useless and futile—I felt like a god, ready to crush these feeble insects in my powerful hand, to grind these entangled vipers under my heel; and I laughed.

Scarcely ten minutes had passed before Robert had not a word left to say. Hubert was doing all the talking. No doubt he was issuing his orders; and the other assented with little nods of his head, and I saw his submissive shoulders getting rounder and rounder. Alfred, for his part, lounging on his straw-seated chair as though it were an armchair, with his right foot cocked up on his left knee, had tilted himself backwards, with his head thrown back; and I could see his fat, shining face, bilious and black-bearded, upside down.

Finally they got up. I followed them, keeping in concealment. They walked slowly, Robert in the middle, hanging his head, as though he were wearing handcuffs. Behind his back, his coarse red hands plucked at a soft hat, of a dirty, faded grey.

I thought that there was nothing left to surprise me. I was wrong. While Alfred and Robert went on to the door, Hubert plunged his hand into the holy water font, turned towards the high altar, and made a large sign of the Cross.

I was in no hurry now. I could take my time. What was the use of following them? I knew that that very evening, or the next day, Robert would at last press me to carry out my plans.

How should I receive him? I had plenty of time to think about it. I was beginning to feel tired. I sat down.

For the time being, what was uppermost in my mind, what suppressed everything else, was the feeling of irritation caused by Hubert's action. A girl, of modest bearing and not much to look at, put a hat-box down on the floor beside her and knelt down in the row of chairs in front of mine. I saw her in profile, with her head a little bent, her eyes fixed on that same distant little door which Hubert, his family duty accomplished, had just so gravely saluted. The girl smiled a little, and did not stir.

Two seminarists entered in their turn, one of them very tall and very thin, who reminded me of Abbé Ardouin; the other short, with a face like a doll. They knelt down side by side, and they, too, seemed stricken into immobility.

I looked at what they were looking at; I tried to see what they were seeing. "In fact," I said to myself, "there is nothing here but silence, coolness, and the smell of old stones in shadow." Again the face of the little milliner's assistant attracted my attention. Her eyes were closed now; her lids, with their long lashes, reminded me of those of Marie on her death-bed.

I felt at one and the same time quite close, within reach of my hand, and yet at an infinite distance away, an unknown world of goodness. Often Isa had said to me: "You, who see nothing but evil. . . . You, who see evil everywhere. . . ." It was true, and it was not true.

Chapter XVI

I had lunch quite light-heartedly, almost gaily, in a state of well-being such as I had not known for a long time, just as though Robert's betrayal, instead of upsetting my plans, worked to their advantage.

A man of my age, I said to myself, whose life has been threatened for years, does not seek remote reasons for his ups and downs of humour. They are organic. The myth of Prometheus signifies that all the sorrows of the world have their seat in the liver. But who dare proclaim a truth so lowly?

I was not in pain. I digested my underdone slice of broiled meat. I rejoiced that the helping was generous enough to save the expense of getting something else as well. I should have some cheese to follow: the most nourishing thing, at the cheapest possible price.

What attitude should I adopt towards Robert? I must change the direction of my fire. But I could not fix my mind on these problems. In any case, what was the good of restricting myself to a fixed plan? It was much better to rely upon the inspiration of the moment. I did not dare to admit what pleasure I promised myself in playing, like a cat, with that wretched country mouse. Robert was a thousand miles from suspecting that I had unearthed the mine. . . .

Am I cruel? Yes, I am. Not more than anybody else, than all the others, than children, than wives, than all those (I am thinking of the little milliner's girl whom I glimpsed at Saint-Germain-des-Prés) than all those who are not on the side of the Lamb.

I went back in a taxi to the Rue Bréa, and lay down on

my bed. The students who populate that boarding-house were on holidays. I could take my rest in complete calm. Nevertheless, the glass half-door, covered with a dirty screen, deprived that room of any intimacy. Several little wood-carvings of the Henri II bed had come unstuck, and were carefully assembled in the bronze-gilt waste-basket which adorned the fireplace. Sheaves of stains displayed themselves on the shining, watered wall-paper. Even with the window open, the smell of the ornate night-table, with its red marble top, filled the room. A cloth with a mustard ground covered the table.

The whole setting pleased me as a microcosm of human ugliness and pretentiousness.

The rustle of a skirt awakened me. Robert's mother was standing at my bedside, and the first thing I saw was her smile. Her obsequious air would have sufficed in itself, even if I had not known anything, to put me on my guard and warn me that I had been betrayed. A certain kind of politeness is always a signal of betrayal.

I smiled back at her, and assured her that I was feeling better. Her nose had not been so gross, twenty years before. At that time she possessed, by way of population for her mouth, those fine teeth which Robert has inherited from her. But to-day her smile shone out over a complete set of false teeth.

She must have been walking fast, and the acrid odour of her strove victoriously with that of the table with the red marble top. I begged her to open the window as widely as possible. She did so, came back to my side, and smiled at me again.

Now that I was feeling better, she wanted to tell me that Robert put himself at my disposal, for "the business." As it happened, the next day, Saturday, from noon onwards, he would be free. I reminded her that on Saturday afternoons the banks were shut. Then she said that he could get leave on Monday morning. He would have no difficulty about obtaining it. In any case, he need not worry about his employers any longer.

She seemed surprised when I insisted that Robert should hold on to his job for the next few weeks. She took her leave with the assurance that she would accompany her son to see me the next day. I begged her to let him come by himself; I wanted to talk to him a little, to get to know him better. . . .

The poor fool could not conceal her anxiety. She was afraid, no doubt, that her son would give himself away. But when I speak with a certain air, nobody dreams of disputing my decisions. It was unquestionably she who had pushed Robert into coming to an understanding with my children. I knew that timid, fearful fellow too well to have any doubts about the uneasiness into which the step that he had taken must have plunged him.

When the wretch came in, during the morning of the next day, I saw at the first glance that my expectations were surpassed. His eyes were those of a man who has not slept. The way in which they looked at one was shifty. I bade him sit down, and was concerned about his appearance. In short, I showed myself affectionate, almost loving.

I described to him, with all the eloquence of a great lawyer, the life of felicity that opened before him. I evoked the house and the ten-hectares park which I was going to buy for him at Saint-Germain. It was going to be furnished throughout in "period" style. There would be a fish-pond, a garage for four cars, and lots of other things which I threw in as ideas came into my head.

When I talked to him about the cars, and suggested to him one of the leading American makes, I saw a man in agony. Clearly he was under contract not to take a half-penny while I was alive.

"You need not worry about this," I told him; "the transaction will go through under your own name. I have set aside, with the object of handing them over to you on Monday, a certain number of securities which will give you an income of a hundred thousand francs a year. Even with that, you needn't care what happens. But most of the liquid fortune is still in Amsterdam. We might make a trip there next week, to put all our affairs in order. . . . But what's the matter with you, Robert?"

"No, Monsieur, no," he stammered, "nothing before your death. . . . I really wouldn't like it. . . . I don't want to deprive you of anything. Please don't insist; you're only hurting me."

He was leaning up against the wardrobe, with his left elbow in his right hand, rubbing himself against the corners. I fixed upon him those eyes of mine which used to put so much dread into my adversary at the Law Courts, and, when I was the advocate of the injured party, never left my victim until he collapsed in the witness-box into the arms of a policeman.

At bottom, I forgave him. I experienced a sense of deliverance. It would have been terrible to end my days with that larva. I did not hate him. I intended to throw him away without hurting him. But I could not restrain myself from playing with him a little longer.

"What fine feelings you have, Robert! How nice it is of you to be ready to wait until I am dead! But I cannot accept such a sacrifice on your part. You shall have it all, starting on Monday; by the end of the week the greater part of my fortune will be in your name."

He was about to protest.

"It's a case of take it or leave it," I added, coldly.

Refusing to meet my eyes, he asked me for a few days more to think it over. Just time to write to Bordeaux and get his instructions, poor fool!

"You surprise me, Robert, I must say. This attitude of yours is strange."

I thought I was looking less fierce; but my eyes are sterner than I am myself. Robert stammered in a ghost of a voice:

"Why are you staring at me like that?"

I mimicked him despite myself as I replied:

"Why am I staring at you like that? And you—why can you not look me in the face?"

Those who have the habit of being loved instinctively do all the things, and say all the words, that attract people. And I—I am so used to being hated and making people afraid that my pupils, my eyebrows, my voice, my laugh make themselves the obedient accomplices of this awful gift of mine and act in advance of my will. So the wretched fellow wriggled about under a stare which I wanted to express forgiveness. The more I laughed, the more the sound of that mirth impressed itself upon him as a sinister omen.

Just as one finishes off an animal, I questioned him point-blank.

"How much did they offer you, the others?"

I addressed him in the familiar second person singular, and that familiarity, whether I intended it or not, conveyed more contempt than friendliness. He stammered: "What others?"—a prey to an almost holy terror.

"The two gentlemen," I told him, "the fat one and the thin one . . . yes, the fat one and the thin one."

I wanted to make an end of it. I felt a horror of prolonging the scene—just as when one dare not put his heel on a centipede.

"Pull yourself together," I said to him finally. "I forgive you."

"It wasn't I who wanted to do it . . . it was . . ."

I put my hand over his mouth. I could not have endured to hear him accusing his mother.

"Hush! No names! . . . Come now, how much did they offer you? A million? Half a million? Less than that? It's not possible! Three hundred thousand? Two hundred thousand!"

He shook his head piteously.

"No, an annual income," he said in a low voice. "That

147

was what tempted us. It was safer. Twelve thousand francs a year."

"Starting from to-day?"

"No, starting from when they got the inheritance. . . . They hadn't foreseen that you would want to put everything in my own name at once. . . . But is it too late? . . . It's true that they could prosecute us . . . unless we hide ourselves from them. . . . Oh, what a fool I've been! I am well punished. . . ."

He cried—an ugly sight—sitting on the bed; one of his hands hung down, huge, swollen with blood.

"After all, I am your son," he sobbed. "Don't let me down!"

With an awkward movement, he tried to throw his arms round my neck. I freed myself, but gently. I went over to the window, and spoke to him without turning round.

"You will receive, beginning on August 1, fifteen hundred francs a month. I shall take immediate steps to have this income paid to you for life. If you die before her, your mother will have the reversion of it. My family, of course, must not know that I discovered the plot at Saint-Germain-des-Prés." The name of the church made him jump. "I need not tell you, at the least indiscretion on your part, you will lose everything. In return, you will keep me informed of anything that may be planned against me."

He knew now that nothing had escaped me, and what it would cost him to betray me again. I gave him to understand that I did not want to see either him or his mother again. They were to write to me *poste restante*, at the usual post-office.

"When are they leaving Paris, your accomplices of Saint-Germain-des-Prés?"

He assured me that they had taken the evening train the day before. I cut short his show of gratitude and his promises. No doubt he was stupefied. A fantastic divinity, whose ways were unforeseeable, and whom he had betrayed, laid hands upon him, let him go, picked him up again. . . . He shut his eyes and opened his mouth. With his tail between his legs, and his ears flattened, he carried away on all fours the bone that I tossed him.

Just as he was going out, he thought better of it and asked me how he would receive this income, through what medium.

"You will receive it," I told him coldly. "I always keep my promises. Nothing else is any business of yours."

With his hand on the latch, he still hesitated.

"I would rather it were a life interest, an annuity, something like that, in a sound insurance company. . . . I should feel more comfortable, I shouldn't worry so much. . . ."

I wrenched the door that he was holding wide open, and pushed him out into the passage.

Chapter XVII

I leant against the mantel-piece, and mechanically counted the pieces of varnished wood assembled in the waste-basket.

For years I had dreamt of this unknown son of mine. All through my poor life, I had never lost the feeling that he existed. Somewhere there was a child, born of me, whom I could find again and who, perhaps, would comfort me.

The fact that he was of humble condition made him all the closer to me. It was pleasant to me to think that he would be in no way like my legitimate son. I endowed him at one and the same time with that simplicity and that power of attraction which are not rare among the common people.

Finally I had played my last card. I knew that, after him, I had nothing left to expect from anybody, and that there would be nothing for me to do but curl up and turn my face to the wall. For forty years I had believed that I accepted hatred: that which I inspired, that which I felt. But, like other people, I cherished a hope, and I had deceived my hunger, as best I could, until I was reduced to my last resource. Now it was finished.

There did not remain to me even the frightful pleasure of laying plans to disinherit those who had wronged me. Robert had put them on the track. They would certainly end by discovering my safes, even those which were not in my own name.

Think of something else? Oh, if only I could go on living, and have the time to spend it all—and die, and leave them with not enough to find to pay for a pauper's burial! But after a whole life of saving, when I had made myself a slave to my passion for economy for years, how was I to learn, at my age, the ways of the prodigal?

Besides, the children are watching me, I said to myself. I should never be able to do anything in that direction without its becoming a formidable weapon in their hands. . . . I should have to ruin myself furtively, little by little. . . .

Alas! I should never be able to ruin myself. I should never succeed in losing my money. If only it were possible to take it with me into the grave, to go back to earth holding that gold, those notes, those securities in my arms! If only I could give the lie to those who preach that this world's riches do not follow us into death!

There were "good works"—"good works" are pitfalls which swallow up everything. Could I not send anonymous gifts to the Board of Charity, to the Little Sisters of the Poor? Could I not, in short, think of others—others besides my enemies?

But the horror of old age is that it is the sum-total of a life—a sum-total of which one cannot change a figure. I have spent sixty years creating this old man dying of hatred. I am what I am. I should have to become somebody else. Oh God, oh God—if only You existed! . . .

At dusk a girl came in to turn down my bed. She did not close the shutters. I lay down in the dimness. The noises of the street, the light of the lamps, did not prevent me from drowsing. I came back to consciousness momentarily, as one does on a journey when the train stops; then I dozed off again. Though I did not feel any worse, it seemed to me as though I had nothing to do but lie there and wait patiently until this sleep became eternal.

I had still, however, to take steps for the payment of the promised income to Robert, and I also wanted to go to the *poste restante*, since there was nobody to do me this service now. For three days I had not had any letters. That expectancy of an unknown letter, that expectancy which survives everything—what a sign it is that hope cannot be up-rooted, and that there is always some of that weed left in us!

It was this eagerness about my letters that gave me the strength to get up the next day, about noon, and go to the post-office. It was raining, I had no umbrella, and I hugged the walls. My appearance aroused curiosity, and people turned round to look at me.

I felt like shouting at them: "What is there odd about me? Do you take me for a madman? You mustn't do that—the children will take advantage of it. Don't look at me like that. I am the same as everybody else—except that my children hate me and that I have to defend myself against them. But that's not the same thing as being mad. Some times I am under the influence of all the drugs I have to take for my angina pectoris.

"Well, yes, I do talk to myself, because I am always alone. Speech is necessary to a human being. Why should there be anything odd about what a lonely man does or says?"

The packet which was handed to me contained some printed matter, some letters from the bank, and three telegrams. Probably they were about some Stock Exchange transaction which could not be carried through. I waited until I was seated in a cheap restaurant before opening them.

At long tables some bricklayers, looking like clowns of all ages, were slowly eating their due portions and drinking their pints, scarcely talking at all. They had been working in the rain all the morning. They had to start again at half past one. It was the end of July. Everybody was flocking to the stations. . . .

Would they understand anything about my torture? Of course they would!—and how could an old lawyer imagine anything else? The very first case in which I had appeared concerned children disputing among themselves about keeping their father. The wretched man went from one to another, every three months, cursed by all of them—and he was at one with his children in clamouring for death to deliver him from them. On how many peasants' farms had I not witnessed that tragedy of the old man who, for a long time, refuses to relinquish his property, and then lets himself be done out of it, with the result that his children kill him with over-work and under-feeding?

Yes, he ought to know all about it, that thin, gnarled bricklayer a couple of yards away from me, slowly munching his bread between his toothless gums.

Nowadays a well-dressed old man in a cheap restaurant excites no remark. I dissected a piece of whitish rabbit, and amused myself by watching the rain-drops trickling together on the window. I deciphered the name of the proprietor the wrong way round. I felt for my handkerchief, and my hand encountered the packet of letters.

I put on my glasses, and opened one of the telegrams at random. "Mother's funeral to-morrow July 23 nine o'clock church Saint Louis." It was dated that morning. The other two, sent the day before, must have followed one another at a few hours' interval. One read: "Mother very ill return": the other: "Mother dead. . . ." All three were signed by Hubert.

I crumpled up the telegrams and went on eating. My mind was preoccupied with the thought that I should have to find the strength to take the night train. For some minutes I thought of nothing else. Then another feeling came to life in me: astonishment at surviving Isa.

It was understood that I was going to die. That I was to be the first to go was a matter about which there was no question, either for myself or for anybody else. Plans, intrigues, plots—all had no object other than the days which were to follow my death, very near at hand. I did not entertain the smallest doubt on the subject, any more than my family.

There was an aspect of my wife of which I had never

lost sight. It was that of my widow, a woman whose crape would be in her way when she opened the safe. A change of the stars in their courses could not have caused me greater perturbation, greater uneasiness, than this death of hers. Despite myself, the man of business in me started examining the situation and deciding what attitude to adopt towards my enemies. Such were my feelings until the moment the train started.

Then my imagination came into play. For the first time, I saw Isa as she must have been in her bed, yesterday and the day before. I reconstituted the setting, her room at Calèse—I did not know that she had died at Bordeaux. I murmured: "putting her in the coffin . . ." and gave way to a cowardly sense of relief.

What would my attitude have been? How should I have borne myself under the watchful, hostile eyes of the children? Those questions did not arise now.

For the rest, the bed to which I should have to betake myself as soon as I arrived would avoid any difficulties. There could be no question of my being present at the funeral; at that moment I had just made an effort to reach the lavatory, in vain.

This weakness of mine did not frighten me. Now that Isa was dead, I no longer expected to die; my turn had passed. But I was afraid of an attack, more especially as I was alone in my compartment. Somebody would meet me at the station—I had telegraphed—Hubert, no doubt. . . .

No, it was not he. What a relief when I saw the fat face of Alfred, strained with lack of sleep! He seemed frightened at the sight of me. I had to take his arm, and I could not get into the car without his help. We drove to my house in Bordeaux, cheerless under a rainy morning, through a district of slaughter-houses and schools.

I had no need to talk. Alfred went into the smallest details, and described the precise spot in the public gardens where Isa had collapsed (just before you come to the greenhouses, in front of the clump of palm-trees); the chemist's shop to which she had been carried; the difficulty of getting a woman of her weight up to her room, on the first floor; the blood-letting, the tapping. . . .

She had remained conscious all night, despite cerebral hæmorrhage. She had asked for me by signs, insistently, and then she had fallen asleep, just as a priest arrived with the blessed oils. "But she had received Communion the day before. . . ."

Alfred wanted to drop me at the house, already draped in black, and go on himself, on the ground that he had barely time to change for the funeral. But he had to resign himself to helping me out of the car. He assisted me up the steps.

I did not recognise the hall. Within its shadowy walls, groups of candles were burning around a heap of flowers. I blinked my eyes. The sense of being somewhere else which I felt resembled that of certain dreams. Two motionless nuns had been provided together with everything else. From that collection of draperies, flowers and lights the usual staircase, with its worn carpet, ascended towards everyday life.

Hubert came down it. He was in evening dress, very correct. He held out his hand to me and spoke; but from what a distance his voice came! His face approached mine, and grew enormous, and then I lost consciousness.

They told me afterwards that this faint of mine lasted only three minutes. I came to myself in a little room which used to be the waiting-room, before I gave up the Bar. Smelling-salts pricked my mucous membrane. I recognised Geneviève's voice: "He's coming round. . . ."

I opened my eyes. They were all bending over me. Their faces seemed to me different, disfigured, red, some of them greenish. Janine, healthier than her mother, looked as old as she did.

Tears had ravined Hubert's face especially. He had that ugly, touching expression that he used to have as a child,

at the time when Isa took him on her knee and said to him:
"He's very sorry for himself, isn't he, my little boy? . . ."
Only Phili, in that evening suit which he had dragged
through all the night-haunts of Paris and Berlin, showed
me on his handsome face indifference and boredom—looking just the same as, no doubt, he did when he went out on
a party, or rather when he came back, drunk and di-
shevelled; for he had not yet tied his tie.

Behind him, I could just make out some veiled women,
who must have been Olympia and her daughters. Other
white shirt-fronts gleamed in the shadows.

Geneviève put a glass to my lips, and I took a few sips.
I told her that I was feeling better. She asked me, in a
gentle, kindly voice, whether I would like to go and lie
down at once. I spoke the first words that came into my
head.

"I should have liked so much to accompany her to the
end, since I was not here to say 'Good-bye' to her."

I repeated, like an actor trying to get the right key: "Since
I was not here to say 'Good-bye' to her"; and these commonplace words, intended only to save appearances, which
came to me because they were a part of my rôle in the
funeral rites, awakened in me, with sudden power, the feeling of which they were the expression.

It was as though I had told myself something which I
had not yet realised. I should never see my wife again.
There would never be any explanation between us. She
would never read these pages. Things would remain eter-
nally at the point where I had left them when I went away
from Calèse.

We could not begin over again, make a start on a new
basis. She was dead without knowing me, without knowing that I was not merely that monster, that torturer, and
that another man existed in me. Even if I had arrived at
the last moment, even if we had not exchanged a word, she
would at least have seen the tears that now furrowed my

cheeks; she would have carried away with her the vision of my grief.

Only my children, mute with astonishment, contemplated that spectacle. Probably they had never seen me cry, in the whole of their lives. That old, surly, terrifying face, that Medusa's head whose stare none of them had ever been able to withstand, metamorphosed itself, became simply human. I heard somebody saying (I think it was Janine):

"If only you hadn't gone away! . . . Why did you go?"

Yes, why had I gone away? But could I not have got back in time? If the telegrams had not been addressed to me *poste restante,* if I had received them at the Rue Bréa. . . . Hubert was rash enough to add:

"Going away like that without leaving any address. . . . We had no idea . . ."

A thought, hitherto confused in my mind, came to birth all at once. Supporting myself with my two hands on the arms of the chair, I got up, trembling with rage, and shouted straight in his face: "Liar!"

He stammered: "Father, have you gone mad?" and I went on:

"Yes, you are all liars. You knew my address. Dare to tell me to my face that you did not know it!"

Hubert protested feebly: "How could we have known it?"

"Were you not in contact with anybody in close touch with me? Dare to deny it—just dare!"

The family, frozen into stone, stared at me in silence. Hubert shook his head like a child entangled in its own lie.

"You didn't pay him very much for his betrayal, either. You were not very generous, my children. Twelve thousand francs a year to a fellow who gives you back a fortune— it's next to nothing."

I laughed—that laugh which makes me cough. The children could not find a word to say. Phili muttered, half to himself: "Dirty trick. . . ." I went on, lowering my voice in response to a beseeching gesture from Hubert, who was vainly trying to speak.

"It is because of you that I did not come back in time. You kept in touch with everything I was doing, but you could not let me suspect it. If you had telegraphed to the Rue Bréa, I should have known that I was betrayed. Nothing in the world would have made you do that—not even the supplications of your dying mother. It hurt you, no doubt, but you kept your eyes on the main chance. . . .

I said all this to them, and other things even more horrible. Hubert implored his sister: "Get him to stop! Get him to stop! They'll hear him . . ." in a gasping voice. Geneviève put her arm round my shoulders and made me sit down again.

"This isn't the time for all this, Father. We'll talk about it later on, when we've slept on it. I beg of you, in the name of her who is still here. . . ."

Hubert, livid as a corpse himself, put a finger to his lips. The master of ceremonies came in with a list of the people who were to be pall-bearers. I took a few steps forward. I wanted to walk by myself. The family scattered in front of me as I tottered along. I succeeded in crossing the threshold of the mortuary chapel and sinking down on a kneeling-stool.

There Hubert and Geneviève came to fetch me. They took me one by each arm, and I went with them obediently. Getting up the staircase was a difficult business. One of the nuns agreed to look after me during the funeral. Hubert, before he left me, affected to ignore what had passed between us, and asked me whether he had done right in naming the President of the Bar Council as a pall-bearer. I turned my face towards the streaming window, without taking the trouble to reply.

Already there was the noise of many feet. The whole town was coming to pay its respects. On the Fondaudège side, with whom were we not allied? And, on my side, there were the Bar, the banks, the business world. . . .

I felt a state of well-being, like that of a man who has been let off, whose innocence has been recognised. I had convicted the children of lying. They had not denied their guilt.

While the whole house still murmured, as though this were some strange ball without music, I forced myself to fix my mind upon their crime. It was they alone who had prevented me from receiving Isa's last farewell. . . .

But I spurred my old hatred like a jaded steed. It made no response. Physical prostration, or satisfaction at having had the last word—I do not know what it was that made me more gentle, despite myself.

The sound of the appropriate prayers came to my ears no longer. The noise of the funeral died away in the distance, until a silence as deep as that of Calèse reigned in the vast house. Isa had emptied it of its inhabitants. Behind her corpse she had carried away with her the whole household. There was nobody left but myself and the nun, finishing at my bedside the rosary that she had begun beside the coffin.

That silence made me once more sensitive to the eternal separation, to the departure from which there was no coming back. Again there was a choking in my throat, because, now, it was too late, and between her and me there was nothing more to say.

Sitting up in bed, propped up with pillows, to help my breathing, I looked at that Louis XIII furniture, whose model we had chosen at Bardié's, while we were engaged, and which had been hers until the day when she had inherited her mother's furniture. It was that bed, that sorrowful bed, of our resentments and our silences. . . .

Hubert and Geneviève came in alone, while the others stayed outside. I realised that they could not get accustomed to my face in tears. They stood at my bedside: the brother looking incongruous in his evening dress in broad daylight; the sister a pillar of black from which a white handkerchief emerged, with her veil, thrown back, revealing a face like a round of boiled beef. Grief had unmasked us all, and we could not recognise one another.

They asked how I was feeling. Geneviève said:

"Nearly everybody came to the cemetery. She was very much loved."

I inquired about the days that had preceded her attack of paralysis.

"She wasn't feeling well. . . . Perhaps, indeed, she had a presentiment; for, the day before she went to Bordeaux, she spent a lot of time in her room, burning a heap of letters. In fact, we thought the chimney was on fire."

I interrupted her. A thought had struck me. . . . Why had it not occurred to me before? . . .

"Geneviève, do you think my going away had anything to do with it?"

She answered me, with an air of satisfaction, that "no doubt it was a blow to her."

"But you hadn't said anything to her . . . you hadn't told her about what you had discovered? . . ."

She questioned her brother with her eyes. Was she supposed to understand? I must have looked terrible at that moment, for they seemed frightened. While Geneviève helped me to sit up, Hubert replied hastily that their mother had fallen ill more than ten days after my departure, and that, during that period, they had decided to keep her out of these unhappy discussions. Was he telling the truth? He added, in a quavering voice:

"Indeed, if we had succumbed to the temptation of telling her, we should be the first to be responsible. . . ."

He turned away a little, and I could see his shoulders moving convulsively. Somebody pushed the door ajar, and demanded to know if they were ever going to have lunch. I heard Phili's voice: "What about it? I can't help it if I'm starving. . . ."

Geneviève asked me, through her tears, what I would like to eat. Hubert said that he would come back after lunch. The matter must be cleared up, once and for all, if I felt equal to it. I nodded acquiescence.

When they had gone, the nun helped me to get up, and I was able to have a bath and drink a bowl of beef-tea. I did not want to engage in this battle as a sick man whom the enemy would treat with chivalry and consideration.

When they came back, it was to find a different man from that old man who had aroused their pity. I had taken the necessary drugs. I was sitting straight up in my chair. I felt less oppressed, as I always do when I leave my bed.

Hubert had changed into a morning suit; but Geneviève was wrapped in an old dressing-gown of her mother's. "I have nothing black to put on." They sat down facing me; and, after a few conventional words, Hubert began.

"I have thought about this a good deal. . . ."

He had carefully prepared his speech. He addressed me as though I were a meeting of shareholders, weighing every word carefully, anxious to avoid any unpleasantness.

"At my mother's bedside, I made my examination of conscience. I forced myself to change my point of view and put myself in your place. A father who is obsessed with the idea of disinheriting his children—that is how we regard you, and that is what, in my eyes, justifies or at least excuses all our conduct. But we have given you a point against us by our lack of consideration in the struggle and by our. . . ."

As he was hesitating over the right word, I suggested to him gently: " 'By our cowardly plots.' "

His cheeks flamed. Geneviève protested.

"Why 'cowardly'? You are so much stronger than we are. . . ."

"Come, come! A very ill old man against a young pack! . . ."

"A very ill old man," Hubert retorted, "enjoys a privileged position in a house like ours. He does not leave his room, he remains on the watch there, he has nothing to do but observe the habits of the family and turn them to his advantage. He makes his plans by himself, and has leisure to prepare them. He knows everything about the others, who know nothing about him. He knows the listening-posts. . . ."

Here I could not help smiling, and they smiled too.

"Yes," Hubert went on, "a family are always imprudent. We argue, we raise our voices. Everybody ends by shouting without realising it. We trusted too much to the thickness of the walls of this old house, forgetting that its ceilings are thin. And then there are open windows. . . ."

These allusions created a kind of relaxation of tension between us. Hubert was the first to revert to a serious tone.

"I admit that we may have appeared to blame. I repeat that it would be child's play for me to invoke the argument of legitimate defence; but I want to avoid anything which might embitter this discussion. Nor shall I seek to decide who was the aggressor in this unhappy quarrel. I will even agree to plead guilty to that. But you must understand. . . ."

He stood up. He polished the lenses of his glasses. His eyes blinked in his lined, haggard face.

"You must understand that I was fighting for the honour, for the very life, of my children. You cannot imagine our position. You belong to another century. You have lived in that fabulous period when every prudent man invested in safe securities. I know very well that you were equal to circumstances, that you saw the storm coming before anybody else, that you realised in time. . . . But it was just because you had retired, because you were outside the business—that's the way to put it! You could estimate the situation in cold blood, you could master it, you were not in it up to the neck as I am. . . . The awakening was too sudden. . . . This is the first time that all the branches have given way at once. One can't hold on to anything, get a grip on anything. . . ."

How desperately he repeated: "anything . . . anything.

. . ."! How deeply was he committed? On the verge of what disaster was he struggling?

He was afraid that he had given himself away, and went back on his tracks and gave vent to the usual commonplaces: the specialisation of industrial equipment after the war, over-production, the crisis in consumption. . . . What he said mattered little. It was to his attitude that I paid attention.

At that moment, I realised that my hatred was dead—and that my desire for revenge was dead with it. It had been dead, perhaps, for a long time. I had stoked up my resentment, I had spurred myself on. But what was the good of refusing to look facts in the face?

I experienced, in the presence of my son, a confused feeling in which curiosity was uppermost. The agitation of the poor fellow, his terror, his anxiety that I could relieve with a single word—how strange that seemed to me! I saw in my mind's eye that fortune which had meant, apparently, everything in life to me; which I had sought to give away, to lose; which I had not even been free to dispose of as I liked—that thing from which quite suddenly, I felt myself detached, which did not interest me any more, did not concern me any more.

Hubert, now silent, peered at me through his glasses. What was I devising? What blow was I going to deal him? He was already setting his teeth, drawing himself up, half-raising his arm like a child protecting itself. He went on in a timid voice.

"All I ask of you is that you should straighten out my affairs. With what will be coming to me from Mamma, I shall not need"—he hesitated a moment before naming the sum—"more than a million francs. Once the ground is cleared, I can get on my feet again all right. Do what you like with the rest; I undertake to bow to your wishes. . . ."

He swallowed his saliva; he looked at me furtively; but I maintained an impenetrable expression.

"But you, my daughter," I said, turning to Geneviève,

"you are all right? Your husband is a shrewd fellow. . . ."

Praise of her husband always irritated her. She protested that his business was finished. He had not been buying any rum for the past two years. In that way he was sure of not making a mistake! Of course they had enough to live on; but Phili was threatening to leave his wife, and was only waiting to make sure that the fortune was lost.

I muttered: "Good riddance!" and she went on quickly:

"Yes, he's a rotter, we know that, and Janine knows it too . . . but, if he leaves her, it will kill her. You can't understand that, Father. It's not in your line. Janine knows more about Phili than we do ourselves. She has told me often that he's worse than anything we can imagine. That won't prevent her from dying if he leaves her. That may seem absurd to you. Things like that don't exist for you. But, with your great intellect, you can understand things that you don't feel."

"You're tiring Papa, Geneviève."

Hubert was thinking that his heavy-handed sister was "making a bloomer," and that I was hurt in my pride. He could see signs of pain in my face; but he could not possibly appreciate the cause of it. He did not know that Geneviève was opening an old wound and digging her fingers into it.

I sighed: "Lucky Phili!"

My children exchanged a glance of astonishment. In all sincerity, they had always regarded me as half-mad. Perhaps they would have had me put away with quite easy consciences.

"A bad lot," groaned Hubert, "and he's got us."

"His father-in-law is more indulgent than you are," I said. "Alfred often says that Phili 'isn't such a bad kind of idiot'."

Geneviève flared up.

"He's got Alfred, too. The son-in-law has corrupted the father-in-law. It's well known in the town. People often meet them together, going about with girls. . . . What a disgrace! That was one of the things that worried Mamma. . . ."

Geneviève dabbed at her eyes. Hubert thought that I was trying to distract their attention from the essential thing.

"But that's not what we are talking about, Geneviève," he said, in a tone of irritation. "One would think that there was nobody but you and your family in the world."

She protested furiously that she "would like to know who was the more selfish of the two of them." She added:

"Naturally we all think of our own children first. I have done everything for Janine, and I'm proud of it, just as Mamma did everything for us. I'd throw myself into the fire. . . ."

Her brother interrupted her, in that sharp tone which I recognised as my own, to say that she "would throw other people too."

How such a dispute would once have amused me! I should have hailed with joy the signs foreshadowing a merciless battle over the few bits of heritage which I could not succeed in snatching from them. But I felt rather disgusted, rather bored. . . . Let this question be settled once and for all! Let them leave me to die in peace!

"It is strange, my children," I said to them, "that I should end by doing what always seemed to me the greatest folly. . . ."

Oh, they did not think about squabbling any longer! They turned hard, distrustful eyes towards me. They waited. They put themselves on guard.

"I, who had always kept before my eyes the example of the old peasant, deprived of his property, whom his offspring allow to die of hunger. . . . And, when he is too slow about it, they pile eiderdowns on him, cover him right up to his mouth. . . ."

"Father, I beg of you. . . ."

They protested with an expression of horror which was not assumed. I changed my tone suddenly.

"You are going to be busy, Hubert. Sharing-up will be a difficult business. I have deposits all over the place, here, in Paris, abroad. And then the land, the buildings. . . ."

At every word their eyes grew rounder and rounder; but they refused to believe me. I saw Hubert's thin hands open wide and close again.

"Everything must be finished before my death, at the same time as you divide up what comes to you from your mother. I reserve for myself the use of Calèse, the house and the park—maintenance and repairs to be at your expense. About the vineyards, you can do what you like. A monthly income, of which the amount remains to be settled, will be paid to me by the lawyer. . . . Pass me my note-case . . . yes, in the left-hand pocket of my jacket."

Hubert passed it to me with a hand that trembled. I took an envelope out of it.

"You will find here some notes about the whole of my fortune. You may take it to Arcam, the lawyer. . . . No, better still, telephone to him to come here. I will give it to him myself, and confirm my dispositions in your presence."

Hubert took the envelope, and asked me, with a look of anxiety:

"You're not playing the fool with us, are you?"

"Go and telephone to the lawyer. You'll soon see whether I am playing the fool with you. . . ."

He hastened to the door; then he stopped.

"No," he said, "it would hardly be the thing to do to-day. . . . We ought to wait for a week."

He passed his hand over his eyes. Clearly he was ashamed; he was forcing himself to think of his mother. He turned the envelope over and over.

"All right," I interjected, "open it and read it; I give you permission."

He went quickly over to the window and slit open the envelope. He read as though he were eating. Geneviève, unable to restrain herself any longer, got up and stretched over her brother's shoulder a greedy head.

I looked at that fraternal couple. There was nothing there

for me to regard with horror. A business man threatened with ruin, the father and the mother of a family, had suddenly rediscovered millions which they had thought lost. No, they did not strike me as horrible.

But my own indifference astonished me. I resembled a patient coming out of an operation, who awakens and says to himself that he has felt nothing. I had torn out of myself something to which I was attached, so I thought, by the deepest roots. But I felt nothing but relief, a physical lightening. I breathed more easily.

After all, what had I been doing, for years, except trying to get rid of that fortune, load it upon somebody who was not of my own family? I have always been mistaken about the object of my desires. We do not know what we desire. We do not love what we think we love.

I heard Hubert saying to his sister: "It's enormous . . . it's enormous . . . it's an enormous fortune." They exchanged a few words in low voices; and then Geneviève declared that they would not accept my sacrifice, that they did not want to deprive me of everything.

Those words "sacrifice," "deprive" sounded strangely in my ears. Hubert was insistent.

"You are acting under the influence of the emotion of to-day. You think yourself more ill than you are. You are not yet seventy. People live to be very old with a trouble like yours. After a little time you will be sorry. I will relieve you of all business anxieties, if you like. But keep what belongs to you in peace. We want nothing more than what is just. We have never sought anything but justice. . . ."

Fatigue possessed me, and they saw my eyes close. I told them that I had made up my mind, and that I would talk no more about it except in the presence of the lawyer. They had already reached the door when I recalled them, without turning my head.

"I forgot to tell you that a monthly income of fifteen hundred francs is to be paid to my son Robert. I promised it to him. Remind me of that when we draw up the agreement."

Hubert blushed. He did not expect that arrow. But Geneviève saw no malice in it. Round-eyed, she made a rapid calculation and said:

"Eighteen thousand francs a year. . . . Don't you think that's a lot?"

Chapter XVIII

THE meadow is brighter than the sky. Smoke goes up from the earth, gorged with water, and the cart-ruts, full of rain, reflect a muddy blue. Everything still interests me just as it did in the days when Calèse belonged to me. Nothing is mine any more, and I do not feel my poverty.

The sound of the rain, at night, on the rotting grape-harvest gives me no less concern than when I was the master of this threatened crop. The fact is that what I took for a sign of attachment to the property is merely the carnal instinct of the peasant, son of peasants, born of those who, for centuries, have anxiously scanned the sky.

The income which I am supposed to get every month will go on accumulating at the lawyer's. I have never had any need of it. I have been a prisoner all my life long to a passion which did not possess me. As a dog barks at the moon, so I was fascinated by a reflection.

Imagine waking up at sixty-eight—being born again on the point of dying! May I be given a few years more, a few months, a few weeks! . . .

The nurse has gone. I feel much better. Amélie and Ernest, who looked after Isa, now look after me. They know how to make injections. Everything is ready at hand: bottles of morphine, nitrate.

The children are so busy that they scarcely ever leave the town, and reappear here only when they need my opinion about a valuation. . . . Everything is passing off without too many disputes. Their terror of being "disadvantaged" has made them take the comic decision to divide the complete sets of damask linen and glassware. They would cut a tapestry in two rather than let any one of them have the benefit of it. They would spoil everything rather than let one share be greater than another.

This is what they call "having a passion for justice." They have spent their lives masking the lowest instincts under fine names. . . . No, I ought to strike that out. Who knows whether they are not prisoners, as I was myself, to a passion which does not belong to the part of their nature that is deepest?

What do they think about me? That I have been beaten, no doubt, that I have surrendered. They have "got me." Still, at every visit they show me great respect and gratitude. All the same, I surprise them. Hubert especially keeps me under observation; he distrusts me, he is not sure that I am disarmed.

Reassure yourself, my poor boy. I was not very formidable even that day when I came back convalescent to Calèse. But now. . . .

The elms along the roads and the poplars in the meadows make up two broad surfaces, one above the other, and between their sombre lines the mist gathers—the mist and the smoke of bonfires, and that immense breath of earth after it has drunk. For we find ourselves suddenly in the middle of the autumn; and the grapes, on which a little moisture remains caught and shining, will never recover that of which the August rains robbed them.

But for us, perhaps, it is never too late. I have to keep on telling myself that it is never too late.

It was not out of devotion that, the day after my return here, I went into Isa's room. Mere idleness, that complete lack of occupation which I never know whether I like or dislike in the country—that alone moved me to push open the unlatched door, the first at the top of the staircase, to the left. Not only was the window wide open, but so, too, were the wardrobe and the cupboard. The servants had swept the place clean, and the sun devoured, even in the remotest corners, the impalpable remains of a destiny that was finished.

The September afternoon buzzed with awakened flies. The thick, round lime-trees looked like damaged fruit. The blue, deep at the zenith, paled towards the sleeping hills. A trill of laughter burst from a girl whom I could not see; sun-hats moved about at the level of the vines; the grape-harvest had begun.

But the miracle of life had departed from Isa's room; and at the back of the cupboard a pair of gloves, an umbrella, had the air of dead things. I looked at the old stone chimney-piece which carries, sculptured on its tympan, a rake, a spade, a sickle and an ear of corn. These old-time chimneys, in which great logs can burn, are blocked during the summer by big screens of painted canvas. This one represented a yoke of labouring oxen. One day, when I was a little boy, I had slashed it with a pen-knife in a fit of temper.

It was only leaning against the chimney. As I was trying to settle it in its proper place, it fell forward and revealed the black square of the hearth, full of ashes. Then I remembered what the children had told me about that last day of Isa's at Calèse. "She was burning papers; we thought there was a fire. . . ."

I realised, at that moment, that she had felt death coming. One cannot think about his own death and other people's at one and the same time. Obsessed by the idea of my approaching end, how could I have worried about Isa's high blood pressure? "It's nothing—just old age," those fools of children kept on saying.

But she, that day when she made that big fire, knew that her hour was at hand. She had wanted to disappear entirely. She had effaced the least vestiges of herself. I stared, in the hearth, at those grey embers, that the draught barely stirred. The tongs that she had used were still there, between the hearth and the wall. I seized them, and foraged in that heap of dust, in that nothingness.

I dug into it, as though it concealed the secret of my life, of our two lives. In proportion as the tongs penetrated into them, the ashes became harder. I assembled a few fragments of paper which the thickness of the leaves had protected; but I rescued only odd words, broken phrases, whose meaning was impenetrable.

They were all in the same handwriting, which I barely recognised. My trembling hands applied themselves to the task. On a tiny fragment, dirtied with soot, I was able to make out this word: PAX. Beneath a little cross was a date: "February 23, 1913," and: "my dear daughter. . . ."

Out of other fragments I attempted to reconstitute the characters that were written on the margin of the burned page; but all that I obtained was this: "You are not responsible for the hatred which this child inspires in you. You would be to blame only if you yielded to it. But on the contrary you drive yourself. . . ."

After repeated efforts, I succeeded in reading this much more: ". . . judge the dead harshly . . . the affection that he has for Luc does not prove . . ." Soot covered the rest, except these sentences: "Forgive without knowing what you have to forgive. Offer for him your. . . ."

I should have time to think it over later. I had no other thought but that of finding something more. I went on foraging, bending over, in a position which stopped my breathing. At one moment the discovery of a moleskin note-book, which appeared to be intact, excited me; but none of its leaves had been spared. On the verso of the cover, I could make out only these few words in Isa's handwriting: *Spiritual Nosegay;* and, underneath: "I am not called He Who condemns, My name is Jesus." (*Christ to Saint Francis de Sales*).

Other quotations followed, but they were illegible. In vain did I bend for long over that dust; I could obtain nothing more. I straightened myself up and looked at my blackened hands. I saw, in the glass, my brow smeared with ashes. A desire for walking took possession of me, as in the days when I was young. I went downstairs, forgetful of my heart.

For the first time for weeks, I made my way towards the vines, half-stripped of their fruits, which were nodding into sleep. The country-side was volatile, limpid, airy as those bluish balloons that Marie once used to blow up at the end of a straw. Already the wind and the sun were hardening the cart-ruts, the deep imprints of the oxen.

I walked on, bearing with me the image of that unknown Isa, a prey to strong passions which God alone had possessed the power to master. That housewife had been a sister eaten up by jealousy. Little Luc had been hateful to her . . . a woman capable of hating a little boy . . . jealous because of her own children? Because I preferred Luc to them? But she had hated Marinette. . . .

Yes, yes, she had suffered through me. I had possessed the power to torture her. What madness this was! Marinette was dead, Luc was dead, Isa was dead—dead, dead! And I, an old man still on my feet, but on the brink of that grave into which they had gone down—I rejoiced in the fact that a woman had not been indifferent to me, that I had stirred these depths in her.

It was laughable; and, indeed, laugh I did, all to myself, leaning against a vine stake, face to face with the wan waste of mist in which villages with their churches, roads and all their poplars, were swallowed up. The light of the setting sun blazed a difficult trail through that buried world.

I felt, I saw, I had it in my hands—that crime of mine. It did not consist entirely in that hideous nest of vipers— hatred of my children, desire for revenge, love of money; but also in my refusal to seek beyond those entangled vipers. I had held fast to that loathsome tangle as though it were my very heart—as though the beatings of that heart had merged into those writhing reptiles.

It had not been enough for me, throughout half a century, to recognise nothing in myself except that which was not I. I had done the same thing in the case of other people. Those miserable greeds visible in my children's faces had fascinated me. Robert's stupidity had been what struck me about him, and I had confined myself to that superficial feature. Never had the appearance of other people presented itself to me as something that must be broken through, something that must be penetrated, before one could reach them.

It was at the age of thirty, or at the age of forty, that I should have made this discovery. But to-day I am an old man with a heart that beats too slowly, and I watch the last autumn of my life putting the vines to sleep, stupefying them with smoke and sunshine.

Those whom I should have loved are dead. Dead are those who might have loved me. As for the survivors, I no longer have the time, or the strength, to set out on a voyage towards them, to discover them. There is nothing in me, down to my voice, my gestures, my laugh, which does not belong to the monster whom I set up against the world, and to whom I gave my name.

Was it exactly these thoughts that I was going over in my mind, as I leant against that vine stake, at the end of a vineyard, opposite the slopes resplendent with Yquem, on which the declining sun rested? An incident, which I must record here, doubtless made them clearer to me; but they were in me already, that evening, while I made my way back to the house, steeped to my very heart in the peace that filled the earth.

The shadows lengthened. The whole world was nothing but an acceptation. In the distance, hills lost in the gloaming looked like bowed shoulders. They were awaiting the mist and the night, perhaps to lie down, and stretch themselves, and fall into a human sleep.

I hoped to find Geneviève and Hubert in the house. They had promised to have dinner with me. It was the first time in my life that I looked forward to seeing them, that I found enjoyment in it. I was impatient to show them my new heart.

I must not lose a moment in getting to know them, in making myself known to them. Should I have time to put my discovery to the test before I died? I would go straight to the hearts of my children, I would pass through everything that had separated us. The tangle of vipers was at last cut through. I should advance so quickly into their love that they would weep when they closed my eyes.

They had not arrived. I sat down on a bench, near the road, listening for the sound of a car. The longer they delayed, the more I wanted them to come. I had a return of my old bad temper. Little they cared about keeping me waiting! What did it matter to them if I suffered on their account? They did it on purpose. . . .

I pulled myself up. Their lateness might be due to some reason which I did not know, and it was not likely that it was the precise reason whereby, through force of habit, I nurtured my resentment. The bell rang for dinner. I went to the kitchen to tell Amélie that we had better wait a little longer.

It was very rare for me to be seen under those blackened rafters from which hams hung. I sat down beside the fire, in a wicker chair. Amélie, her husband and Cazau, the handy man, whose loud laughter I had heard in the distance, had fallen silent as soon as I came in. An atmosphere of respect and terror surrounded me.

I never talk to servants. It is not that I am a difficult or exacting master; they simply do not exist in my eyes, I never even notice them. But this evening their presence comforted me. Because my children had not come, I was quite ready to have my meal at a corner of the kitchen table, where the cook was carving the joint.

Cazau took himself off, and Ernest put on a white jacket to wait on me. His silence oppressed me. I tried to find something to say. But I knew nothing about these two people who had devoted themselves to us for the past twenty years. Finally I remembered that their daughter, married at Sauveterre in Guyenne, used to come and see them, and that Isa did not pay her for the rabbit she brought, because she had some meals in the house. I spoke rather quickly, without turning my head.

"Well, Amélie, how is your daughter? Still at Sauveterre?"

She bent her weather-beaten face towards me and stared at me.

"Monsieur knows that she is dead. . . . It will be ten years on the 29th, Saint Michael's Day. Surely Monsieur remembers?"

Her husband, for his part, said nothing, but he looked at me sternly. He thought that I was pretending to have forgotten. I stammered: "I beg your pardon. . . . my old head. . . ." But, as always when I am shy and embarrassed, I chuckled a little—I could not help chuckling. The man announced, in his usual voice: "Dinner is served."

I got up at once, and went and sat down in the dining-room, opposite the shade of Isa. Here was Geneviève, then Abbé Ardouin, then Hubert. . . . I looked, between the window and the sideboard, for Marie's high chair, which had served for Janine and for Janine's daughter. I endeavoured to swallow a few mouthfuls. The stare of that man who waited on me was horrible to me.

In the drawing-room they had lit a fire of vine-branch faggots. In that room every generation as it withdrew had left, as a tide leaves its shells, albums, caskets, daguerreotypes, astral lamps. Dead knick-knacks littered the tables. The heavy stamp of a horse in the darkness, the sound of the wine-press that adjoins the house, almost broke my heart.

"My little ones, why didn't you come?" The moan rose to my lips. If the servants had heard me through the door, they must have believed that there was a stranger in the drawing-room; for this could not be the voice, or the words, of the old wretch who, they imagined, had pretended on purpose not to know that their daughter was dead.

All of them, wife, children, masters and servants, had formed a conspiracy against my soul. They had dictated this hateful rôle to me. I had painfully adopted the attitude which they demanded of me. I had conformed to the model which their hatred laid down for me.

What madness, at sixty-eight, to hope to swim against the stream, to impose upon them a new idea of the man that, nevertheless, I am, that I always have been! We only see what we are accustomed to seeing. You, too, my poor children, I do not see you either.

If I were younger, the lines would be less marked, the habits less deeply rooted; but I doubt whether, even in my youth, I could have broken the spell of this enchantment. One needed some strength, I said to myself. What kind of strength? Someone.

Yes, Someone in Whom we are all one, Who would be the guarantor of my victory over myself, in the eyes of my family; Someone Who would bear witness for me, Who would have relieved me of my foul burden, Who would have assumed it. . . .

Even the elect do not learn to love all by themselves. To get beyond the absurdities, the failings, and above all the stupidity of people, one must possess a secret of love which the world has forgotten. So long as this secret is not rediscovered, you will change human conditions in vain.

I thought that it was selfishness which made me aloof from everything that concerns the economic and the social; and it is true that I was a monster of seclusion and indifference; but there was also in me a feeling, an obscure certitude, that all this serves for nothing to revolutionise the face of the world. The world must be touched at its heart. I seek Him Who alone can achieve that victory; and He must Himself be the Heart of hearts, the burning centre of all love.

I felt a desire which perhaps was in itself a prayer. I was

on the point, this evening, of falling on my knees, with my arms on the back of a chair, as Isa used to do, in those summers of long ago, with the three children pressing against her skirts. I used to come back from the terrace towards that illuminated window, walking silently and, invisible in the dark garden, look at that group at prayer. "Prostrate before You, O my God," Isa would recite, "I give You thanks that You have given me a heart capable of knowing You and loving You. . . ."

I remained standing in the middle of the room, hesitating, as though I had been hit. I thought of my life; I contemplated my life. No, one could not swim against such a stream of mud. I had been a man so horrible that I had never had a single friend.

But, I said to myself, was it not because I had always been incapable of disguising myself? If all men went through life as unmasked as I had done for half a century, perhaps one would be astonished to find how little difference in degree there was among them.

In fact, nobody goes through life with his face uncovered —nobody at all. Most people ape highmindedness, nobility. Unknown to themselves, they are conforming to types, literary or otherwise. The saints know this: they hate and despise themselves because they see themselves as they really are. I should not have been so despised if I had not been so frank, so open, so naked.

Such were the thoughts that pursued me, this evening, as I wandered about the dimly lit room, where I stumbled against a heavy piece of furniture of mahogany and rosewood, a piece of jetsam sanded up in the past of a family, where so many bodies, to-day returned to dust, had sat and lain stretched. Children's boots had dirtied the divan when they buried themselves in it to look at the *Monde Illustré* in 1870. The stuff was still black at the same place. The wind prowled round the house, laying flat the dead leaves of the lime-trees. They had forgotten to close the shutters of a bedroom.

Chapter XIX

THE next day, I awaited the arrival of the postman anxiously. I paced up and down the walks, as Isa used to do when the children were late and she was worried.

Had they quarrelled? Was one of them ill? I fretted myself to death. I became as clever as Isa at developing and harbouring obsessions. I marched among the vines, with that absent-minded air of remoteness from the world of those who are going over and over a source of anxiety; but, at the same time, I remember that I noticed this change in myself, and was pleased to find that I was anxious.

The mist was a sound-box. One could hear the plain, but not see it. Wag-tails and thrushes made merry in the rows where the grapes had not yet gone rotten. Luc as a child, at the end of his holidays, had loved these fleeting mornings. . . .

A line from Hubert, dated from Paris, did not reassure me. He had been obliged, he told me, to leave in a hurry: a rather serious matter which he would tell me about on his return, fixed for the next day but one. I imagined financial difficulties. Had he, perhaps, been guilty of some illegality?

By the afternoon I could not stand it any longer. I had myself driven to the station, where I took a ticket for Bordeaux, though I had given my word not to travel alone again. Geneviève was now living in our old house. I met her at the door, in the act of taking leave of a stranger, who must have been a doctor.

"Didn't Hubert tell you?"

She took me into the waiting-room, where I had fainted, the day of the funeral. I breathed again when I heard that it was a matter of an escapade of Phili's. I had feared something worse. He had gone off with a woman "who had a hold on him," after a distressing scene in which he had left Janine with no hope. They could not get the poor girl out of her state of prostration, which worried the doctor. Alfred and Hubert had followed the fugitive to Paris. According to a telegram which she had just received, they could do nothing with him.

"When I think that we allowed them such a large income. . . . Of course we weren't taking any risks; we did not give them control of any capital. But the income was considerable. God knows Janine showed herself weak enough with him; he could get anything he liked out of her. When I think that he used to threaten to desert her, because he believed that you would not leave us anything; and it's now, when you have handed over your fortune to us, that he makes up his mind to take off—how do you explain that?"

She stopped in front of me, with her brows arched and her eyes dilated. Then she went and leant against the radiator, put her finger-tips together, and rubbed her hands.

"Of course," I said, "it's a rich woman in the case. . . ."

"Not at all!—a teacher of singing. . . . But you know her yourself; it's Mme Vélard. Not in her first youth, and no better than she should be. How do you explain that?" she repeated.

She started talking again without waiting for my reply. At that moment Janine came into the room. She was in her dressing-gown. She put up her forehead for me to kiss. She was no thinner; but in that heavy, graceless face despair had wiped out everything that I disliked. This poor creature, so affected, so mannered, had become terribly stark and simple. The harsh light of a lamp fell full upon her without her blinking an eye. "You know?" was all she asked me; and she went and sat down on the *chaise-longue*.

Did she listen to her mother's conversation, that interminable harangue which Geneviève must have been dinning into her ears ever since Phili's departure?

"When I think. . . ."

Every period began with this "When I think," astonishing in a person who thought so little. They had consented to this marriage, she said, despite the fact that at the age of twenty-two Phili had already dissipated a nice fortune which he had inherited very young—as he was an orphan, without near relations, he had had to be released from trusteeship. The family had closed their eyes to his life of debauchery . . . and this was the way in which he rewarded them. . . .

An irritation was coming to life in me which I tried to control in vain. My old maliciousness opened an eye again. As though Geneviève herself, Alfred, Isa, all their friends, had not harried Phili, had not dazzled him with promises by the thousand!

"The most curious thing about it," I growled, "is that you really believe what you are saying. But you know perfectly well that you all ran after the fellow."

"Come, come, Father, you're surely not going to defend him. . . ."

I protested that there was no question of defending him. But we had been wrong in thinking this fellow Phili even lower than he really was. No doubt it had been rubbed into him too much that, once the fortune was assured, he would put up with anything and there would be no more danger of his taking himself off. But people are never as bad as we think they are.

"When I think that you defend a wretch who deserts his young wife and his little daughter. . . ."

"Geneviève," I cried in exasperation, "you misunderstand me. Make an effort to understand me. To abandon one's wife and daughter is a bad thing, that goes without saying; but the culprit might have yielded to baser motives rather than to higher ones. . . ."

"So then," repeated Geneviève, aghast, "you think noble to desert a woman of twenty-two and a little girl. . . ."

There was no getting her beyond that. She simply did not understand what I was talking about.

"No, you're too much of a fool . . . unless you refuse to understand on purpose. . . . All I am saying is that Phili appears to me less despicable since. . . ."

Geneviève cut me short, crying to me to wait until Janine had left the room before insulting her by defending her husband. But the girl, who so far had not opened her lips, intervened in a voice which I barely recognised.

"Why deny it, Mamma? We treated Phili as though he were lower than dirt. You remember, once the division was decided upon, we thought we had him where we wanted. Yes, he was just like a dog which I was to keep on a lead. I had reached the point where I ceased to suffer because he didn't love me. I had him; he was mine; he belonged to me; I held the purse-strings; I had the whip-hand over him. It was your own expression, Mamma. Remember that you said to me: 'Now you have the whip-hand over him.'

"We thought that he wouldn't put anything above money. Perhaps he thought so himself; but in the end his resentment, his sense of humiliation, were too much for him. It isn't as though he loved this woman who has taken him away from me. He told me so when he was going away, and he threw so many cruel things in my face that I'm sure he was speaking the truth. But she didn't despise him; she didn't lower him in his own eyes. She gave herself to him, she didn't take him. But I—I was offered to him."

She repeated these last words, as though she were flagellating herself. Her mother shrugged her shoulders, but she was glad to see her in tears. "That will do her good.

"Don't be afraid, my dear," she went on; "he'll come back to you. Hunger drives the wolf out of the woods. When he has roughed it long enough. . . ."

I was sure that sentiments such as these aroused Janine's disgust. I got up and picked up my hat. I could not bear to spend the evening with my daughter. I gave her to understand that I had hired a car and that I would drive back to Calèse. Suddenly Janine said:

"Take me with you, Grandfather."

Her mother asked her whether she had gone mad. She must stay where she was. The lawyers wanted her. Besides, at Calèse, "grief would get the better of her."

On the landing, where she followed me out, Geneviève reproached me heatedly because I had encouraged Janine's passion for Phili.

"If she succeeds in getting rid of that fellow, confess that it would be a good riddance. One can always find grounds for annulment of marriage; and, with her fortune, Janine could make a brilliant match. But, in the first place, she must get him out of her system. And you, who used to detest Phili—you go out of your way to sing his praises in front of her! . . . Oh no, above all things she must not go to Calèse. You would send her back to us in fine shape! Here, we shall succeed in taking her mind off it in the end. She will forget. . . ."

Unless she dies, I thought; or unless she lives a life of misery, with a pain that is always the same, over which Time is powerless. Perhaps Janine belongs to that race of women whom an old lawyer knows well: those women in whom hope is a disease, who are never cured of hoping, and who, after twenty years, still keep looking at the door, with the eyes of a faithful dog.

I went back to the room where Janine was still sitting, and I said to her:

"Any time you like, my child. . . . You will always be welcome."

She showed no sign of having understood me. Geneviève came back and asked me suspiciously: "What are you saying to her?" I heard afterwards that she accused me of having, during those few seconds, "perverted" Janine and amused myself "by putting all kinds of ideas into her head."

But I went down the staircase, treasuring in my memory what the girl had said to me: "Take me with you . . ."

She had asked me to take her with me. I had said, instinctively, about Phili just what she needed to hear. I was
the first person, probably, who had not hurt her.

I walked about Bordeaux, luminous in a day of harvest-
home. The pavements of the Cours de l'Intendance, damp
with mist, were shining. The voices of noon drowned the
clamour of the trams. The smell of my childhood was missing. I might have found it again in those more sombre dis-
tricts of the Rues Dufour-Dubergier and de la Grosse
Cloche. There, perhaps, some old woman, at the corner of
a dark street, still clutched to her bosom a steaming pot of
those boiled chestnuts which smell of aniseed.

No, I was not melancholy. Somebody had listened to me,
understood me. We had come together. That was a victory.
But I had failed with Geneviève: there is nothing that I
can do against a certain quality of stupidity. One can readily
reach a living soul behind the saddest of faults and failings;
but vulgarity is insurmountable.

No matter, I would make up my mind to it: one could
not roll away the stone from all these tombs. I should be
very happy if I succeeded in penetrating just one soul, before I died.

I slept at a hotel, and did not return to Calèse until the
following afternoon. A few days afterwards, Alfred came to
see me, and I learnt from him that my visit had had unhappy results.

Janine had written Phili a crazy letter, in which she declared that all the faults were on her side, blamed herself,
and asked his forgiveness. "Women never do anything but
the wrong thing. . . ." My fat friend did not dare to say it
to my face, but he was certainly thinking: "She is beginning her grandmother's follies over again."

Alfred gave me to understand that any suit was lost in
advance, and that Geneviève held me responsible for the
fact. I had purposely made Janine pig-headed. I asked my
son-in-law, with a smile, what my motives could possibly

have been. He told me—protesting that he did not agree with his wife's opinion in the least—that I had acted, according to her, out of malice, for revenge, perhaps through "sheer wickedness."

The children did not come to see me any more. A letter from Geneviève informed me, a fortnight later, that they had had to send Janine to a nursing home. There was no question of her being mad, of course. They had great hopes of this isolation cure.

And I, too—I was isolated; but I was not in pain. Never had my heart given me such a long respite. During this fortnight and well beyond it, a radiant autumn lingered in the world. No leaf had fallen yet, and the roses bloomed again.

I ought to have suffered because, once more, my children shunned me. Hubert put in an appearance only to talk business. He was cold and correct. His manner remained courteous, but he kept himself on his guard. The influence which my children accused me of having won over Janine had made me lose all the ground I had gained. I had become once more, in their eyes, the enemy, a treacherous old man, capable of anything. Finally, the only one who might have understood me was shut up, segregated from the living.

And yet, I experienced a sense of profound peace. Bereft of everything, isolated, living under a terrible threat of death, I remained calm, interested, active-minded. The thought of my sad life did not overwhelm me. I did not feel the weight of those wasted years. . . .

It was as though I were not a very ill old man; as though I still had before me a whole lifetime; as though this peace which possessed me were Someone.

Chapter XX

THOUGH it is a month since she fled from the nursing home and I took her in here, Janine is not yet cured. She believes that she was the victim of a plot. She declares that she was shut up because she refused to take proceedings against Phili for divorce and annulment of her marriage. The others imagine that it is I alone who put these ideas into her head and set her against them; whereas in fact, in the course of these interminable days at Calèse, I have been fighting step by step against her illusions and her chimeras.

Outside the rain mingles the leaves with the mud and rots them. Heavy clogs crunch the gravel of the courtyard. A man goes by with a sack over his head. The garden is so stripped that nothing any longer hides the insignificance of what is conceded here to the delight of the eyes. The carcases of the hedge-rows, the sparse clumps of bushes, shiver under the eternal rain.

The penetrating damp of the bedrooms robs us of courage to leave the fire in the drawing-room at night. Midnight strikes, and still we cannot resign ourselves to going to bed. The logs, patiently piled up, crumble into ashes. In the same way I have to begin, over and over again, persuading the girl that her parents, her brother, her uncle, do not mean her any harm. I turn her thoughts away from the nursing home as much as I can.

Always we come back to Phili. "You cannot imagine what kind of man he was. . . . You cannot possibly tell how. . . ."

These phrases herald, indifferently, a harangue or a dithyramb, and only her tone enables me to foresee whether she is going to set him on a pedestal or spatter him with mud. But, whether she glorifies him or vilifies him, the facts which she quotes strike me as irrelevant. Love communicates to this poor woman, so lacking in imagination, an astonishing power of distorting, and of amplifying.

I know him, this Phili of yours—one of those meaningless men whom fleeting youth momentarily invests with a glamour. To this spoilt child, stroked and all expenses paid, you attribute intentions subtle or scoundrelly, premeditated perfidies; but he has nothing but reflexes.

You never understood that it was the very breath of life to him to feel himself the stronger. You should never have "held the whip-hand" over him. There are some kinds of dog that will not sit up and beg; they slink off to other leavings that they can get off the ground.

Not even from a distance does the poor girl know her Phili. What does he represent in her eyes, apart from yearning for his presence, longing for his caresses, jealousy, the horror of having lost him? Without eyes, without a sense of scent, without antennæ, she runs about distractedly looking for him, with nothing to inform her about what the object of her pursuit really is. . . .

Are there such things as blind fathers? Janine is my grand-daughter; but, if she were my own daughter, I should still see her no less clearly for what she is: a creature who can expect nothing from anybody. This ordinary-looking woman, dull, heavy, with that silly voice of hers, is marked with the sign of those who never catch an eye, never arrest a thought.

But still she strikes me as beautiful, as I look at her these nights, with a beauty apart from herself, lent to her by her despair. Is there no man whom this flame might attract? But the poor girl burns away in the dark, in a desert, with no other witness except an old man. . . .

Much as I have pitied her, during these long night watches, I have never tired of contrasting Phili, that fellow like millions of others, just as this common white butterfly resembles all white butterflies—and this frenzy, which he alone had the power to release in his wife, and which, for her, annihilated the world, visible and invisible. Nothing existed any longer, in Janine's eyes, but a male already a little bedraggled, inclined to prefer alcohol to anything else, and to regard love as a job, a duty, a weariness. . . . What a tragedy!

She scarcely glanced at her little girl when she glided into the room at dusk. She kissed the child's curls carelessly. Not that the little one had no influence over her mother; it was on her account that Janine found the strength not to set off in pursuit of Phili—for she was the kind of woman to harry him, to taunt him, to make public scenes. No, I would never have sufficed to restrain her; she stayed because of the child; but she derived from her no consolation.

It was in my arms, on my knee, that the little one took refuge, in the evening, while we waited for dinner to be served. I found once more, in her hair, the scent of a bird, of a nest; it reminded me of Marie. I closed my eyes, with my lips against her head; I restrained myself from holding her little body too close; and I evoked in my heart my lost child.

And, at the same time, it was Luc whom I imagined I was embracing. When she had been playing a lot, her skin had that salty taste of Luc's cheeks, at the time when he used to go to sleep at table, after running about so much. . . . He could not even wait for dessert. He went round the table, putting up to us for our kisses his face drawn with sleepiness. . . .

So I dreamed; and Janine walked up and down the room, marching, marching, pacing her passion back and forth.

I remember one evening when she asked me: "What can I do to stand the pain of it? Do you think I shall ever get over it?"

It was a night of frost. I watched her opening the window, flinging the shutters wide. She bathed her brow, her bosom, in the icy moonlight. I brought her back to the fire; and I, so inexpert in being affectionate—I sat down awkwardly beside her and put an arm round her shoulders.

I asked her whether she had nowhere to turn. "You have your faith?"

"Faith?" she replied distractedly, as though she did not understand.

"Yes," I went on, "God. . . ." She turned a burning face towards me, looking at me with a suspicious air, and finally said that she "could not see the connection. . . ." And when I persisted:

"Of course," she said, "I'm religious. I do my duty. Why do you ask me that? Are you making fun of me?"

"Do you think," I asked, "that Phili is all that you give him credit for?"

She looked at me with that sulky, irritated expression of Geneviève's when she does not understand what one is saying to her, when she does not know what to reply, when she is afraid of a trap. Finally she plucked up courage to say that "all this didn't go together." She didn't like mixing up religion with such things. She was a practising Christian, but that was just why she had a horror of such wrongminded associations of ideas. She performed all her religious duties.

She might have said, in just the same voice, that she paid her taxes. It was precisely what I had execrated all my life —just that, nothing but that. In this crude caricature, this mean parody of the Christian life, I had pretended to find an authentic representation to justify me in hating it.

One must have the courage to look at what one hates straight in the face. But I, I said to myself, I. . . . Did I not know already that I was deceiving myself, that evening at the end of the last century on the terrace at Calèse, when Abbé Ardouin said to me: "You are very good . . ."? Later, I had closed my ears to the words of Marie, as she lay dying.

But, at that bedside, the secret of death and life had been revealed to me. A little girl was dying for me. . . . I had tried to forget. Tirelessly I had sought to lose that key which some mysterious hand always gave back to me, at every turning point in my life—the way Luc looked after Mass, those Sunday mornings, at the hour of the first grasshopper. . . . And this spring again, the night of the hail. . . .

So my thoughts ran, that evening. I remember that I got up, pushing my chair back so violently that Janine started.

The silence of Calèse, at that advanced hour, that thick, almost solid silence, benumbed, stifled her grief. She let the fire die down; and, as the room grew colder, she drew her chair closer and closer to the hearth, until her feet almost touched the ashes. The dying fire drew her hands, her face, towards it. The lamp on the mantel-piece shed its rays upon that heavy, hunched-up woman; and I stumbled about, in the darkness encumbered with mahogany and rosewood. I hovered, impotently, around that lump of humanity, that prostrate body.

"My child. . . ." I could not find the word I sought. That which stifles me, to-night, even as I write these lines; that which makes my heart hurt as though it were going to burst; that love of which, at last, I know the name ador——

Calèse,
December 10th, 193—

MY DEAR GENEVIÈVE,

I shall finish, this week, sorting the papers with which every drawer here is bursting. But it is my duty to communicate to you, without delay, this strange document. You know that our father died at his writing-desk, and that Amélie found him, on the morning of November 24th, with his face against a note-book. It is this that I am sending you, under registered cover.

You will, no doubt, have as much trouble as I have had myself in deciphering it. . . . It is lucky that its writing is too illegible for the servants. Moved by a feeling of delicacy, I had at first intended to spare you the reading of it. Our father, in point of fact, expresses himself about you in extremely hurtful terms.

But have I the right to leave you in ignorance of a document which belongs as much to you as it does to me? You know how scrupulous I am about everything that has to do, directly or indirectly, with our parents' heritage. So I changed my mind.

For that matter, which of us is not badly treated in these malicious pages? They reveal, alas! nothing that we have not known for a long time. The contempt which I inspired in my father embittered my youth. I was long doubtful about myself, I abased myself under that merciless stare. It took me years before I finally realised my own worth.

I have forgiven him, and I would even add that it is, above all, filial duty which leads me to communicate this document to you. For, however you may judge him, it is not to be denied that the figure of our father will appear to you here, despite all the frightful feelings which he exhibits, I dare not say more noble, but at least more human. (I am thinking especially of his love for our sister Marie, and for young Luc, to which you will find here some moving testimony.)

I can better understand, to-day, the grief which he showed beside our mother's coffin, and which astonished us so much. You thought that it was partly assumed. Even if these pages serve only to reveal to you how much feeling subsisted in that implacable man, mad with conceit of himself, they will repay the trouble you take in reading them, painful, for that matter, as you may find it, my dear Geneviève.

What I feel that I owe to this confession, and the benefit which you will derive from it yourself, is the easing of our consciences. I was born scrupulous. Even if I had a thousand reasons for believing myself in the right, the smallest thing sufficed to trouble me. Yes, indeed, moral delicacy carried to the point to which I have carried it does not make life any the easier!

Pursued by the hatred of my father, I adopted no means of defence, even the most legitimate, without experiencing anxiety, if not remorse, as a result. If I had not been the head of the family, responsible for the honour of its name and for our children's patrimony, I would have given up the struggle rather than go through those tearings of the heart, those quarrels with myself, of which you have more than once been a witness.

I thank God that He has granted that these lines of our father's should justify me. In the first place, they confirm all that we already knew about the unscrupulous machinations through which he sought to deprive us of his inheritance. I could not read without a sense of shame those pages where he describes the measures which he devised to keep a check, at one and the same time, upon the lawyer Bourru and that fellow Robert.

Let us throw the mantle of forgetfulness over these shameful scenes. The fact remains that it was my duty, at any cost, to frustrate these abominable plans. I did so, and with a success of which I see no reason to be ashamed. Have no doubt about it, my sister—it is to me that you owe your fortune.

The unhappy man, in the course of his confession, endeavours to persuade himself that the hatred which he felt towards us died away all of a sudden. He prides himself upon an abrupt detachment from this world's goods. (I confess that I could not help laughing at this point.) But pay attention, if you please, to the time of this unexpected change of front. It occurred at the very moment when his plans had gone awry and his illegitimate son had sold us the clue to them.

It was no easy matter to make such a fortune disappear. A scheme which it must have taken him years to bring to a head could not be replaced in a few days. The truth is that the poor man felt his end approaching, and that he had neither the time nor the means to disinherit us by any other method than that which he had conceived, and which Providence enabled us to discover.

Lawyer as he was, he was reluctant to lose his case, either in his own eyes, or in ours. He had the shrewdness—half-unconsciously, I admit—to transform his defeat into a moral victory. He affected disinterestedness, detachment. . . .

Well, what else was he to do? No, that is where I refuse to let myself be taken in, and I am sure that you, with your common sense, will agree that we have no occasion to put ourselves to the expense of admiration or gratitude.

But there is another point where this confession sets my conscience entirely at rest: a point about which I have cross-examined myself with the utmost severity, and without succeeding for a long time, as I may frankly admit to-day, in calming this troublesome conscience of mine. I refer to our efforts—fruitless, so far as that goes—to submit our father's mental condition to the examination of specialists.

I may say that my wife had a great deal to do with making me uneasy about this. You know that I am not in the least in the habit of paying much attention to her opinions; she is the least responsible person in the world. But in this case she dinned into my ears, day and night, arguments some of which, I must confess, disturbed me. She ended by convincing me that this great business lawyer, this shrewd financier, this profound psychologist, was the very personification of mental balance. . . .

No doubt it is easy to make hateful in their own eyes children who set about having their old father shut up lest they should lose their inheritance. . . . You see that I do not mince my words. . . . I spent many a sleepless night, God knows.

Very well, my dear Geneviève, this note-book, especially in its later pages, adduces evidence to prove the intermittent delirium with which the poor man was afflicted. His case strikes me as interesting enough to justify submitting his confession to a psychiatrist; but I regard it as my first duty to divulge to nobody pages so dangerous for our children. And I may say at once that, in my opinion, you ought to burn them the very moment you have finished reading them. We ought not to run the risk of their falling under the eyes of a stranger.

You are not ignorant of the fact, my dear Geneviève, that, while we have always kept everything to do with our family very secret—and I have taken precautions lest anything should transpire outside as to our anxieties about the mental condition of him who, after all, was the head of it —certain elements foreign to the family have not used the same discretion or the same prudence. Your wretched son-in-law, in particular, has broadcast the most dangerous stories in this respect.

We are paying dearly enough for this to-day. I am giving you no news when I saw that plenty of people in town see a connection between Janine's neurasthenia and the eccentricities which are attributed to our father, in accordance with Phili's tales.

Destroy this note-book, therefore. Do not say a word about it to anybody. Let there be no further question about it between us. I do not say that this will not be a pity. There are in it pyschological interpretations, and even impressions of Nature, which denote in this orator a real gift for writing. That is all the more reason for destroying it. Suppose one of our children should publish it later on? That would be a nice business!

But, between you and me, we can call things by their own name; and, once we have finished reading this note-book, the fact that our father was half-mad can no longer be in any doubt for us. I understand, to-day, something that your daughter said, which I took for a raving of illness: "Grandfather is the only religious man I have ever met."

The poor girl let herself be taken in by the vague aspirations, the dreamings, of this hypochondriac. Enemy of his own family, hated by everybody, without friends, unhappy in love—there are some amusing details—jealous of his wife to the point of never forgiving her for some sketchy flirtation when she was a girl, did he, towards the end, desire the consolations of prayer?

I do not believe it for a moment. What stares one in the face out of these lines is mental disorder in its most clearly marked form: persecution mania, delirium taking a religious shape.

Is there not any trace, I ask myself, of real Christianity in his case? No; a man as informed as I am about such matters knows that, if you give such people an inch, they take a yard. This false mysticism, I am bound to say, provokes in me an insurmountable disgust.

Is it possible that the reactions of a woman may be different? If this religiosity impresses you, bear in mind the fact that our father, astonishingly endowed as he was for hatred, never loved anything except as a stick with which to beat somebody. His exhibition of his religious aspirations is a criticism, direct or indirect, of the principles which our mother inculcated into us from our childhood. He surrenders himself to a fuliginous mysticism only for the purpose of being better able to attack reasonable, moderate religion, which has always been held in honour in our family. Truth is a matter of balance. . . .

But I stop short of considerations where you would have difficulty in following me. I have said enough. Study the document itself. I am eager to know your impression of it.

I have not much space left to reply to the important questions which you put to me. My dear Geneviève, in the crisis through which we are passing, the problem which we have to solve is agonising. If we keep these piles of banknotes in a safe, we shall have to live on our capital, and that is a misfortune. If, on the other hand, we give our brokers instructions to buy stock, the dividends we get will not recompense us for the uninterrupted decline in capital values.

Inasmuch as we are condemned to lose in any case, it is the wiser thing to keep the Bank of France notes. The franc is only worth four sous, but it is guaranteed by an immense reserve of gold.

On this point our father saw clearly, and we ought to follow his example. There is a temptation, my dear Geneviève, against which you ought to fight with all your strength. It is the temptation of investment at any price, which is so deeply rooted in the French people.

Obviously we must live as economically as possible. You know that you have only to turn to me if you need advice. Despite the bad times, opportunities may present themselves from one day to the next. I am following very closely, at this moment, a cinema and an aniseed liqueur. That is the kind of business which will not suffer from the crisis. In my opinion, it is in such directions that we ought to turn our eyes, boldly but prudently.

I am glad to hear the better news you give me about Janine. There is nothing to be feared, for the moment, in the excess of religious devotion which makes you anxious about her. The essential thing is that her mind should be turned away from Phili. For the rest, she will come back to a sense of proportion by herself. She belongs to a stock which has always known how to avoid abuse of the best things.

Until Tuesday, my dear Geneviève,

Your devoted brother,
HUBERT

Janine to Hubert

MY DEAR UNCLE,

I want to ask you to judge between Mamma and myself. She refuses to entrust Grandfather's "diary" to me. According to her, my regard for him would not survive the reading of it.

If she is so anxious not to hurt my dear memory of him, why does she keep on telling me every day: "You cannot imagine all the bad things he says about you. Even your looks are not spared"? I am the more surprised at her readiness to let me read the harsh letter in which you comment upon this "diary." . . .

Mamma is tired of squabbling about it and says that she will give it to me if you think fit, and that she throws the responsibility upon you. I am therefore making this appeal to your sense of justice.

Allow me, at the outset, to set aside the first objection, which has nothing to do with anybody but myself. However hard upon me Grandfather may show himself in this document, I am sure that he cannot judge me as badly as I do myself. I am sure, above all, that his harshness spares the unhappy girl who lived with him, all autumn, until the day of his death, in the house at Calèse.

Uncle, forgive me if I contradict you on an essential point. I am the sole witness of what Grandfather's feelings became during the last weeks of his life. You denounce his vague and unhealthy religiosity; but I tell you that he had three interviews—one at the end of October and two in November—with the parish priest of Calèse, whose testimony, for some reason which I cannot fathom, you refuse to accept.

According to Mamma, the diary in which he notes the smallest details of his life makes no mention of these meetings—which he would certainly not have omitted to do, if they had been the occasion of a change in his destiny. . . . But Mamma also says that the diary breaks off in the middle of a word. It is unquestionable that death surprised your father just at the moment when he was about to speak of his confession.

It is idle for you to say that, if he had been absolved, he would have received Communion. I know what he kept on telling me, on the day but one before his death. Obsessed by his sense of unworthiness, the poor man had made up his mind to await Christmas.

What reason can you have for not believing me? Why

...make me out a person suffering from hallucination?

..., on the day but one before his death, the Wednesday, I can still hear him, in the drawing-room at Calèse, talking to me about that Christmas for which he longed, in a voice full of pain, or perhaps even then under the shadow of death. . . .

Don't be afraid, Uncle: I am not trying to make a saint out of him. I grant you that he was a terrible man—sometimes, indeed, a dreadful man. That does not alter the fact that a great light shone upon him in his last days, and that it was he, and he alone, who took my head in his two hands, who forcibly made me look another way. . . .

Do you not believe that your father would have been a different man if we had been different ourselves? Do not accuse me of throwing stones at you. I know your good qualities; I know that Grandfather showed himself cruelly unjust towards you and towards Mamma. But it was the misfortune of all of us that he mistook us for exemplary Christians. . . .

Don't protest. Since his death, I have lived with people who may have their defects, their weaknesses, but who live according to their faith, and die in the fullness of grace. If he had lived among them, might not Grandfather have found, after many years, that harbour which he reached only on the eve of his death?

Once more, I make no attempt to discredit our family in favour of its implacable head. I do not forget, above all, that the example of poor, dear Grandmother might have sufficed to open his eyes if, only too long, he had not chosen to be the slave of his resentment.

But let me tell you why, finally, I think that he was right and we were wrong. There where our treasure was, there was our heart also. We thought of nothing but that threatened heritage. No doubt we had plenty of excuses. You were a business man, and I was a poor woman. . . .

That does not alter the fact that, except in the case of Grandmother, our principles remained separate from our lives. Our thought, our desires, our actions struck no roots in that faith to which we adhered with our lips. With all our strength, we were devoted to material things, while Grandfather. . . .

Will you understand me if I tell you that, where his treasure was, there was not his heart also? I would swear that, on this point, the document which you do not want to let me read brings decisive witness.

I hope, Uncle, that you will understand me, and I await your reply with confidence. . . .

JANINE.

IMAGE BOOKS

Image Books constitute a quality library of Catholic writings, broad in human interest and deep in Christian insight. They will include classical Christian writings, devotion, philosophy, education and history; biographies, novels and poetry; and books on contemporary social problems. They represent a planned program of making available to the widest possible audience the finest Catholic literature in attractive, paper-bound, inexpensive editions. They have been selected with these criteria in mind: that they must in every instance be well written, inspiring to the spirit, and of lasting value to the general audience who will purchase them.

The majority of Image Books will consist of reprints made possible through the cooperation of the publishers of the original editions. Occasionally certain much-needed volumes which are not available will also be initiated for this series.

A descriptive catalogue of the Image Books already published may be obtained by writing directly to the publisher. Comments and suggestions from those interested in the series are welcomed by the publisher.